Nancy Luce
In Outer Space

Dr. Charles E. Banks, M.D.

ISBN-13: 9798713398361

Library of Congress Control Number: 2018675309
Printed in the United States of America

NANCY LUCE'S INTERSTELLAR SPACE VESSEL

This recipe is for special occasions when Nancy needs to escape the confines of the Solar System.

Ingredients:
Fifteen thousand plank-feet of oak
Twenty-seven thousand iron rivets
Twelve hundred sheets of waterproof paper
Five hundred barrels of tar
Seven pounds of hempen-twine
Four miles of wire cable
Five hundred square feet of hessian sail-cloth
One quarter-inch steel plate for the heart of the Airship
Three strands of wire for the brain of the Airship
Ten thousand sheets of aluminium for shielding the Airship
Levered pistons to power the Airship
Propellers to push the Airship
Five thousand feet of tethering rope to stay the Airship
Five hundred metres' worth of guide-wires to gird the Airship
Twenty-six thousand polished steel bars to protect the Airship
Three hundred volumes of encyclopedias to fuel the Airship
Two hundred white rats for running along the guide-wires to power and steer the Airship
Thirty Brown Rats to gnaw through any tethering ropes if the Airship is becalmed
Two thousand pounds of yeast to make the Airship rise as it ferments.
Add one Nancy Luce, poet, dreaming of soaring through the stars.
Add salt and pepper to taste.
Warm gently over a fire for exactly nine minutes.
Feast of the gods!

I HAVE DISCOVERED A NEW COLOR

I have discovered a new color, hidden between "red" and "orange". It is difficult to describe, but it is neither reddish nor orangish. Instead, it is more of a "rusty" color, like dried blood. The hue is most marvelous. It is so dark, yet vibrant at the same time! So evocative of mystery and intrigue. I must find a name for this glorious new color. Perhaps I will call it "sanguine", after the Latin word for "blood".

I must go now, and think of a name for this new color. What a marvelous journey that will be! I am filled with hope and contentment, for I have seen the new color, "sanguine", and I am in love with it.

Thank you, dear reader. May God bless you with the gift of literature and a love of words.

Goodbye.

Your humble servant,

Nancy Luce

LAMBERT'S COVE

The folks at Lambert's Cove are peculiar. I won't visit that place any more.They're strange folk. They don't smell like regular humans. They keep to themselves and sometimes speak to one another in an alien language.

I've spoken to a few of them when I had to. They're always nice to me and I appreciate that. But they're just different. Their skin is extremely pale and their eyes don't seem natural.

Anyway, whatever you do just stay away from their houses. As I said, they keep to themselves, but they've probably noticed you already. Be careful! I don't trust them.

My neighbor Samuel moved to Lambert's Cove last year. He doesn't seem like himself any more. I have a feeling he's one of them now.

Anyway, enjoy your stay in West Tisbury. I've been telling people how pretty the area is and encouraging them to visit so maybe this will boost the economy around here a bit.

God bless.

SAUCERS

The saucers have been flying over West Tisbury again. They scare all the livestock.

The nights are getting colder. I wonder when winter will finally come in full. It's been unseasonably cool this year.

I made flapjacks for dinner tonight.

I saw the gray men again, sneaking about in the cornfields by Manter's Farm.

I miss Father.

Tomorrow is Saturday, and that means I shall feed Molob in his pit.

NANCY LUCE'S CHICKEN SURPRISE
This will elicit a jolly laugh from even the most stalwart of eaters!

Ingredients:
one whole chicken, unplucked, cut lengthwise
1 pound marshmallows
1/4 lb. butter
2 eggs
sesame seeds for eyes

Instructions:
Turn the oven to "broil." Place the chicken on a cookie sheet. Unwrap the marshmallows and place them on top of the chicken. Slice the butter and lay it on top of the marshmallows. Broil for 3 minutes, check if done. If not, broil for 2 more minutes. When the marshmallows are golden and bubbly, turn the oven off. Quickly remove the cookie sheet and place it somewhere cool. When the oven is just warm, not hot, crack open the eggs on top of the chicken. Add sesame seeds for eyes. Eat when cooled to room temperature.

Personally, I never eat this dish myself; I find it rather distasteful--however, I have had very peculiar tastes since birth. You might find it "magnifique."

Tip: This recipe reminds one of the nursery rhyme "There Was an Old Lady Who Swallowed a Fly."

Happy cooking!

RED CANNON'S FAILINGS
by Nancy Luce, 1869.

Loud noise. Keep their noise going.
Won't eat blackgrass hay.
Raven for company
Won't come to be milked.
Go dry half their time when with calf.
Kick. Fluk.
Give little milk. Thin milk.
Rank milk. Hold up her milk.
Milk sour quick. Milk hard.
Horns long forward or turn back.
Horns large. Horns sprawl out to sides.
Hook me. Red cow.
Cream go up top in one night, milk not fit to use.
One part of cow large.
Skittish.
Jump. Hook down fence.
Mash down fence.
Run head through fence.
Meet cattle to fence and hook it down and won't come away.
Can't be governed when she has unclean spirit in her.
Short teats.
Bloody milk.
Calf can't nurse.
Scared of calf. Won't let it near her.
Calf can't get milk.
Grass and feed all right. Let down milk.
Haven't had calf to dry up yet but their time coming soon.
Eat rank grass.
Stay hook to barn, leave cow pen door open.
Dirty cow.
One ear point toward ground, one up at sky. Like someone make her mad off and on. Hate me. Watch every move I make. Got devil eye. Angry all the time. Red all over. Want to kill her sometimes. Hate her.

Hate her horns. Hate her mad eye. Hate her mad hooking arm. Hate her mad lifting foot. Mad hooked foot that she drags on the ground. Hate her skittish ways. Hate her wall eye. Hate the other one staring off into the sky. Hate her long teeth that look like devil's own teeth sticking out of her mouth like that. Hate her long white beard. Hate that she's so tall. Hate her sway back. Hate her cow bag, all swollen out and ready to burst some day soon. Hate her tail switched so tight in sky look like it might break any second and lash me with its end any minute.

Hate that she looks at me and won't give milk.

Hate to milk her. Let down socks in rain.

Will let down no matter what.

Fool of an animal.

How did I come to own a vicious animal like her? She's an old scurvy bull that's been laying up in the weeds all summer and fall, eating bad grass and laying around in the hot sun, waiting for winter to kill her. Scraggly, scrannel cow with dirty tail. A wart grew under her belly and another one on her hip. That cow is a disgrace to the entire species. Should've been slaughtered long ago. A beast like that has no business walking on two legs. I hate to see them come into existence in the first place and would encourage the drinking of a strong tea made from the dust of their dried bones ground into powder and dissolved in hot water to create a tonic, or if you're really tough, you can drink it without the tea.

I hate that cow.

Scrawny rat with cloven hooves and a stinking bag of guts around its mouth which it uses to suckle and chew grass like a cow, yet doesn't give milk. That's what a cow is: a rat with cloven hooves and a stinking bag of guts, kept alive just to torment me day after day. To add insult to injury, I have to share my roof with the thing. It's disgusting. Utterly disgusting. I can't stand to even look at it, sleeping there in the corner of my kitchen, chewing its cud all day long. Just looking at the twisted horns on its head makes me nauseous. I'm queasy just looking at that devil's tail, which it insists on swinging around as if to make the very floor vibrate whenever it gets excited.

You want to know what else I hate? I hate cleaning up after that beast.

I hate the foul circuitry that it soldiers, the wiring it lays, the vicious programming that it codes all night. You know how I mentioned I had to milk that menacing, demonic cow? Well, you know what I'm forced to do after I'm done milking it? That's right. I have to clean up after it.

The solder, the fragments of wire, the lead balls, the endless formulae scrawled on my walls. I found a canister of plutonium once it discarded in negligence. Stinking, sloppy cow.

I suppose it's fortunate that I'm a tinkerer, ergo I can easily extract the golden honey from its udders. If I didn't have such a gift for invention, I shudder to think how I'd cope. This is what you need to create hardy machineries of war and death: plasteel, platinum, ceramite, diamonds, deuterium, and last but not least, the humble chicken. They're so full of love. So cuddly.

If I didn't live in perpetual fear that it would wake up and slaughter me in my sleep, I reckon I'd keep one in my bed. I love how they puff up when they're angry. I love the comical way they run inside my hall when it rains. I even love the weirdo dwarven moustache they sometimes grow. They're fascinating creatures, really.

This is what you need to create hardy machineries of war and death: plasteel, platinum, ceramite, diamonds, deuterium, and last but not least, the humble chicken. They're fascinating. I want more of them.

You look skeptical. Surely, you must have heard tales of my creations by now? It is only natural that you wonder if the ravings of a madwoman should be believed, but I assure you, I am not insane. Well, perhaps I am insane, but that does not change the facts. My dreams are real.

You must also be wondering: why a talking chicken? Why not a talking cat, or a talking dog, or even a talking human? Well, because I like chickens. When I was young, my father had a pet chicken who followed me around everywhere when I visited his farm. It was easily the most loyal companion I ever had. My mother hated it, of course.

You want to know something funny? Up until a few years ago, I'd never even eaten chicken. It's just too cowardly and absurd to kill something you know to be intelligent and innocent. Oh, sure, I've killed animals before; we all do it, and what difference does it make to snap the neck of a chicken compared to other, larger, more complex lives? But I knew that if I ever saw one with a face like mine, I would not be able to kill it. All animals are equal, but some are more equal than others. There is something special about chickens; you only need to spend five minutes with one to understand what I mean.

It all began about two years ago when I finally found a reference to an old, abandoned project to create sentient lifeforms out of chicken eggs. The idea was abandoned because none of the test subjects survived long after hatching, let alone reached maturity. Of course, I had to try it myself. I acquired some fertilized chicken eggs from a farmer and set to work. Using the old, forgotten schematics as a guide, I set about modifying the egg with a focus on endowing the chick with human-like intelligence.

I have always been an intellectual, and in many ways this was a perfect project for me. The necessary experiments were neither brutal nor cruel, and they even had the potential to help advance scientific progress. My father always told me never to let fear or morality get in the way of what we want. And I wanted to achieve success with these eggs.

I was extremely cautious at first, but as the eggs began to look promising, I allowed myself to become more and more excited. I would be able to bring a new being into this world. I had already chosen a name, too: Lily Laly.

So enthralled was I by the project that I neglected all else. The final stage of the process was the most important. The newly laid egg must be exposed to high levels of electricity in order to supercharge the dendrite growth in the creature's tiny brain. It would take several weeks at least for the process to be completed, so large was the amount of electrical charge required. The slightest mishap would lead to the egg's destruction, and I refused to risk that.

I had a large, battery-like device installed in the cellar and immersed the eggs in a special solution that would conduct the electricity. Each day I checked on them, praying that none had been damaged during the night.

It was during one of these times that disaster struck. I was descending the stairs when a wooden splinter jabbed into my foot. The pain was sharp, and my yelp was loud. It was so out of character for me that it scared a passing chicken, which flapped its wings madly and knocked over one of the battery's tubes.

That was all it took. There was a bright flash and a loud noise, and then the eggs were destroyed. The contents were horribly burned, and the smell was awful. I cried as I looked at my failed project.

But what I didn't know then was that one egg, while badly damaged, had survived the accident. It looked ruined, with a hole blown through the middle of it and part of the shell burnt black. I picked it up in my hand, noting how light it had become. Turning it over, I was surprised to see a tiny claw, no bigger than a thumbnail, reach out and grab my finger.

I almost dropped the egg, but hesitated. The creature inside seemed to sense I was watching. With a wriggle it pulled itself together and the hole closed up. The shell was still fragile, but had become hard again.

Little did I know what was happening inside that tiny shell that night. I went to sleep awaking in the morning, and for several days I thought I'd just abandoned the experiment.

I found out later that it started then, when the tiny creature shifted inside its egg, a movement so minute I didn't notice. As I write these words it is "born" only a few weeks ago. It drinks the mixture of egg yolk and blood that I provide for it in a small bottle, and wastes no time in developing.

I stare at my tiny monster in wonder.

I named it Lily Laly, for no better reason than it being the first name that came to mind. It appears to have gills like a fish, tiny feet which are developing at an astonishing rate, and fingers which it curls around my little finger when I hold it. It spends all its time sleeping or feeding, and I stay up through the nights making sure that its needs are met quickly.

How can something so small be so demanding? It is very vocal, and whenever it isn't feeding or asleep it is crying out for my attention, "Mmmaaa!" it seems to say. It relies on me for everything. It is not yet known whether it will ever survive without my help, but I think it will be able to. I must keep it safe, and teach it our ways. It is the future of our race, and of our island.

A gentle wind blows over the fields of West Tisbury, rustling through the grass and corn. The Island of Martha's Vineyard is a peaceful place.

Lily Laly has the body of a chicken, but the face of a man. It cries to me. Shh, shh, I say, stroking its face. I hand it another drop of blood on my finger. It happily sucks on it. It's the only thing that stops it from crying.

It only drinks blood now.

It sleeps a lot. It only opens its eyes to feed, and to cry for me.

I stroke its moist, pink skin. Fish-like gills have started to appear on its neck. It opens its eyes slowly as it wakes up. They are a deep blue, like the ocean. I can see them steadily turning darker as the days pass.

It speaks its first word to me: "Doom..." it says.

I smile. "Yes, Lily Laly? Do you need something?"

"Doom..." it says again. It opens its mouth to show me more of its teeth, which are small like a human child's, and still very much like a human child's. I feel its forehead - it has a slight fever. It cries out in pain, and tries to move away from me, but I hold it still.

"Stop, Lily Laly! You'll hurt yourself."

It cries for more than an hour. I caress it slowly as it thrashes against me. I can feel its small, thin muscles under its soft, white skin. Finally, it falls asleep again. Its breathing is shallow. I caress its gills, and its mouth opens slightly. It gently bites my finger. Salty tears well up in my eyes and roll down my cheeks as I hold this strange, beautiful creature in my arms.

I begin to sing it a lullaby my mother sang to me, so many years ago:

West Tisbury is a quiet place
Where fishermen sail and bring back their catches
The Island is ringed by rocky beaches

The little creature bites me, drawing more blood. "Doom..." it says again. I caress it more, and it stops biting. Its gills move slowly, but its black eyes stare blankly ahead.

I sing to it again, a lullaby of my mother's land, Scotland:

Gently screen the light from your eyes my bonnie wee lassie
Night is descending now and the moon soon will rise
Keep the nightmares away that may trouble your slumber
That old hag, Old Nick is coming tonight!
Damn his black soul to Hell, shit-house of pain!
Should he find you slumbering, he'll take your fair soul away.
I've tarried here with you as long as I dare
Lest I suffer the fate of your poor black cat...
Best I disappear lest that bastard should hear
So here's a good-night kiss to send you sweet dreams

The little creature sucks on my finger, removing more blood. "Oxygen..." it says. I smile. I carry my little sea-turtle over to an old chest of drawers and place it in among the folds of my clothing, next to my heart, where it curls up, falling asleep.

The furniture is oak and very heavy. I drag it across the doorway, securing it with chains and a heavy padlock. It's a sorry excuse for a barricade. The thing that hunts me will no doubt shatter it with one attack. It's been tracking me for the past fourteen years... from the barren desert of the future to the ocean-fried island of the past.

It does not give up, it does not stop, and it does not slow. It is a force of nature, like a hurricane. You can see it coming, but there's nothing you can in the end.

My mother called him the "rhyming horror." His true name is long since lost to time, like all things... except myself and him. Other creatures may give him different names, silly things to frighten children with. They lack imagination, though they themselves are far from lacking, horrible freaks of nature that should have been drowned at birth.

For he is no horror. He is beautiful and perfect in his own way, this monster. Imagination is not lacking in him. Oh, how it shines! He is poetry, he is music, he is art! His life is a great work of art, and I am fortunate enough to be the subject of one of his poems.

He does not like me to write about him. He says it is because the false words will not do him justice. I think it is more that he does not wish his identity to be known. The rhyming horror is a criminal, wanted in every port from here to the far future. He murders without a thought, stealing whatever takes his fancy.

But he is so very charming... unlike myself.

The thing about time travel is that everything happens at once. I am writing this in the past, sending it into the far future, where you are reading it. But right now I am also in the future, writing this in the past, sending it back to myself in the present. And right now I am in the past, scribbling this in an old farmhouse on Martha's Vineyard.

And you are there too. You are sitting here, reading my story.

First, you must know that this story is like a block of marble, which I have acquired in the past. It is a block of unpolished marble, dirty and unrefined. But the shape is there. I shall uncover it, refine it, polish it, and make it something of beauty for all to see. I shall make this story of mine something beautiful, a statue for you to marvel.

I am sending you this message from the future. I have travelled back to the 19th century, and you are reading this note in the past, of which I am also writing in the future. Do you understand? I'm afraid that's the only way I can explain it to you.

A time travel device is no simple matter. The first machine was created by an amateur, with no real knowledge of physics or mathematics. I had a device. It was invented by an amateur. I used it many times. It was destroyed. I regret to say it was destroyed by an amateur as well.

The first time I went back in time, it was but a month. The machine was barely functioning, and extremely unreliable. It was but a trial to see if the machine could time travel at all. Miraculously, it did. I travelled back in time 30 months, to find that the past had different ideas than the future. I was still in the hovel I called home. Instead of a derelict ruin overrun by vegetation with my rotting corpse inside, it was fully functioning, although not as I left it. The file said that a professor had bought it, spent good money restoring it, and turned it into a museum of sorts.

Amateur work.

I moved forward in time, and indeed the machine had broken down. I abandoned it. After all, there was no going back now. The future didn't need me any more.

I mostly spent my time in the future, avoiding the past where possible. But curiosity got to me. Before long, I was traveling back as far as a century or so into the past. It's amazing what you can find if you move forward or back in time. Especially in the future.

Where did these notes come from? Oh, from my own time machine, of course. I used it to send them back to myself in the past. It's funny, writing these notes to a younger version of myself. It's nice to see that I've learnt a little about the temporal nature of the universe (That's how we time travelers refer to it. I'm not sure why. "Temporal" just sounds more scientific than "time").

A few notes on the future:

I've avoided using too much future slang and technical jargon, because I'm sending these notes to myself at a younger age. Even I don't know all the words and phrases that will be popular (or not) in the future yet.

I can only hope this information is helpful to my younger self. If you, the reader, find these notes, then either:

a) I have died, in which case please keep them, for they are probably more useful to you than they would be to anyone else.

Or,

b) I have not died, and the future has been too kind to be interesting enough to write about, in which case burn the notes and forget you ever read them.

Either way, goodbye, and thank you for being the only person (or at least the only person I know of) kind enough to reactivate my time machine on that fateful day.

Because of you, I had many happy days.

And that is a debt I can never repay.

The author would like to thank you for reading this story.

NANCY LUCE'S EGGS-AND-MORE-EGGS

This recipe may require an iron stomach.

Ingredients:
Two dozen eggs, each lain by a different bird.
One dozen lamb chops, likewise.
One small barrel of butter.
One gallon milk (churned or raw).
Two ears of corn.
Three loaves of bread (untoasted).
Five pounds of steak (again, untoasted).
Seven sweet red apples (no greens, no bananas).
Nine ripe bananas (make sure they are perfectly ripe).
Mince the twelve chops' worth of lamb, and dice the eggs.
Cut the loaves' worth of bread into slices, then into croutons.
Melt four pounds of butter (but do not scorch it).
N.B. All measurements are of "real world" units, not scientific ones. Use a big bowl for your ingredients -- one usually used for mayonnaise is ideal.

Proceed thusly:
Add in one bowl the chopped lamb, then pour in one pint of melted butter. Stir thoroughly.
Add the mashed bananas and two cups of milk. Stir until blended.
Then add in the shredded wheat, followed by the applesauce. Slowly add in one more pint of melted butter (be careful not to scald yourself). Then pour in the eggs, and fold everything together until somewhat smooth.
Finally stir in the bread crumbs, and pour the whole mess into a casserole dish. Bake at 300 degrees for two to three hours. Spread the loaf of bread with (uncooked) honey, and place slices of it around the edge of the dish as a garnish.
After it has cooled (N.B. Again, to room temperature), cut it into squares and serve with tea. It should last for several days in an airtight container.
Finally, don't forget the salt and the pepper.
N.B. Any sauce will do, so long as it's white.
MEMO: Get cayenne pepper ready, too; sometimes guests request it.
Thanks for the adventure!

MOLOB

Molob sleeps in his pit in West Tisbury, I feed him every Saturday. The rest of the week, he can get by on sheep carcasses. Doubt there's much left to eat on one of those by now, but I toss him one every Saturday just in case. Have to clean up after him too, of course.

I wonder if someday I'll have something more exciting to write about than sheep guts and a giant maggot pit. Perhaps even some interesting people to meet?

Maybe someday.

NANCY'S LUCE'S MENEMSHA MUD BREAD
Earthy and crumbly, as homemade Island bread ought to be.

Ingredients:
4 cups Chilmark mud (strain out and large rocks or roots)
2 cups ea. Bread & Graham Flour
2 tsp. Salt
1 tsp. Sugar
1 1/3 cup Water
Butter (soften), for serving*
Granulated Sugar, for serving*
Finely ground black Pepper, for serving*
Finely chopped fresh Chives, for serving*

Instructions:
Stir together the mud and both flours in large mixing bowl. Stir in salt and sugar.

Add the water and stir together to make a fairly stiff dough.

Cover with damp cloth and let stand for 2 hours (or more).

Turn out on to floured board and knead for 5 minutes.

Form the dough into a ball and let rest, covered with a damp cloth for 15 minutes.

Beat down with flat side of a cleaver or other heavy knife or with flat side of knitters needles.

Let rest covered with damp cloth for 10 minutes more.

Sprinkle top of the dough with flour and cut in half widthwise.

Cut each half widthwise into three strips.

Bend each strip slightly, then roll up from the wide end.

Bend ends of the roll under to form a ring.

Place on well-floured cookie sheet. (Don't use metal—the yeast will make them rise so much they'll stick. If this happens, just chop them up and pretend it was all part of the plan).

Beat the remaining 1 egg in a small dish with a fork and brush tops of the rolls gently with it.

Cover again with damp cloth and let rise until doubled in bulk.

About 20 minutes before ready to bake, preheat the oven to 375°F (190°C).

Bake rolls for 15 minutes, then remove from the oven and rub tops with softened butter, sugar and pepper.

Let cool on wire racks before serving.

Best served fresh.

If you have any left over, they're even better the next day, toasted and slathered in butter and honey.

Add chopped fresh chives.

Excellent paired with Nancy's Luce's Sweet Potato Casserole and Common Cider (recipe found elsewhere in this book).

MOLOB

Saturday, October 11th.

Molob's gone. Took off into the wilderness one morning and haven't seen him since. Probably for the best; this island was obviously not meant to have such a monstrous creature upon it. In fact, I'm writing this to keep myself occupied while I wait for my inevitable death.

Do you remember reading my first journal? The one I wrote when I was but a girl? I've found it again and reread it, as I've been doing a lot of lately. Some of the pages are falling out, and some of the words are harder to make out. But it's like I'm reading about a different person. A happier person.

Maybe I'm just an old crank now, but I've found myself getting angry at that girl for the way she blindly trusted others and had such high hopes for the future.

NANCY LUCE'S TRADITIONAL
WEST TISBURY GAMES

These are the island games Nancy and her friends grew up playing in the 1820s and 1830s in old Tisbury.

1. A merry-go-round of silver and black,
A hawk is hovering above a desperate mouse.
This simple game could last for hours or days,
But all good things come to an end, and so does this ditty.
Who will try their luck at "Hunt the Hawk"?

2. "Rabbit on the Stick", with no tricks at all,
Just a plain old fashioned children's game.
The rules to this game are very easy to learn:
First you need a long, thin piece of wood,
Any child older than six can play this game.
The first player shakes the stick, then each player in turn tries to grab it from the first player, using only their teeth. If they do so, then they become the new first player and shake the stick once more. The game ends when the stick breaks.

3. This is a game that requires a little preparation. You will need two flat stones about the size of saucers, a foot apart. Then you will need a "priest". The priest must stand against a wall and place one foot against it and one on the ground. He then holds the saucer in his hand and throws the other saucer as hard as he can against the wall. He then stops sliding along the floor with his foot and the wall with the saucer. He keeps doing this until someone else catches him doing it. Here is how you play:
One person throws the priest the saucer and says "one". Then he throws it back and says "two", then throws it again,"three", and so on - each time saying the next number after the last number that was said before. When the priest messes up and mixes up the numbers then that person catches the priest doing it. That person becomes the priest. (This is a good game, and can be made more challenging by having the priest put his foot against the wall and hold one of the saucers between his foot and the wall, instead of just using one or the other. You can also play this game with people's shadows, but you must be very skilled to do it that way. You will need a flat surface and a sunny day for that

version of the game.

4. "Kill the Edgartownian". Rules: One player is the "Edgartownian." Then, each player (except the Edgartownian) closes their eyes. The Edgartownian walks around until everyone has had a chance to open their eyes and see where everyone is positioned. Then, they try to tag the other players as quickly as they can. If the Edgartownian tags you, then you become the new Edgartownian.

5. "Tashmoo Poke". For this game, you'll need two sharp knives, a blindfold, a leather strap, and bandages (for any blood.) The two knives should be somewhat flexible, so they can bend. Everyone lines up, with one person in front "It" covers his eyes with the blindfold and holds out the two knives with blades facing outwards. The person behind "It" takes the leather strap and bandages "Its" knife arms to the tops of their arms. Then, everyone follows "It"'s movements by the sound of "Its" knives tapping on the floor. If "It" drops a knife, then everyone has to stop moving and touch the wall. The first person to touch "Its" knives is "It" the next time around. Be careful!
This is a dangerous game that should only be played by people who are experienced with knives.

6. "Jump the Pit" (This game is unique to the Tentacle Pits of Chilmark, and is a highly dangerous game. More than one Vineyard child has been seized and eaten by the creature. You have been warned!)
Rules: One person is sent to the center of the island's largest pit to evade the beast. The rest of the players line up at the edge of the pit and chant a rhyme.
The rhyme goes as follows:

"Blow away, Pit Beast, All covered with hair.
When will you blow away? When will you appear?"

The person in the pit must then quickly move out of the way before a gust of wind blows them into the pit.
If the person survives for one minute, then they have escaped the pit. If not, then they've met a grim fate.

7. "Kookwatcher's Quest"
One person is selected as the Seer. Everyone else forms a circle around the seer, who is placed in the middle of the circle.
The remaining players search for a certain object while the seer tries

to guess who has the object, then everyone switches rolls. It is up to the players to decide whether the search for the object is long or short, easy or difficult. This game can be played as many times as you like, if a player ever gets bored of it, they can make up their own rhyme. But this is the traditional rhyme that is sung:

Up and down the beach strewn with driftwood,
Round and round the maypop stands weeping.
In and out the muckety-muck rushes,
Who carries the sacred key?

8. "The Borderland Fortress". Situate your fort in a clearing in the woods where there is a good source of fresh water. Each fort works independently from each other. No forts are allies. They are all competitors. The forts are competing for land, and whoever has claimed the most territory and defended it successfully by the end of the game wins.

Camp Allamagochie Guidelines: This is the Cuban version, and is most fun when there are large groups of people playing. The goal is to infiltrate the other team's camp and steal their flag while defending your own. The team whose flag has been successfully stolen twice loses.

The Captains (or team leaders) create their teams by selecting who will be on their team. Team leaders may delegate some authority to their team members, but ultimately they are responsible for their team's actions. Each team leader will meet with the other team leaders and determine where the boundaries of the playing field are, where each team's base will be, and an agreed upon time limit. This time limit is flexible. Some days you'll have more time than others. The important thing is to move fast. After the time limit is reached, or everyone is tired of playing, whistle all team members back to their respective base areas. Whistle 3 times and all players must return to their base area immediately.

The Playing Field: There are 2 teams: the Ramblers (derro guerrilleros) and the Wardens (Guardians). Each has a camp and a flag.

9. "Don't Lose Your Eye!" It's always tragic when a child loses an eye. But here's a game that assures that a little fun use can be made of the errant eyeball:

Just tie the lost eye to the end of a kid's wooden broom handle. Let the "Bad Baby" (the one with one eye) chase the other children around the house with his "eye of fate" until someone drops that, then they're "dead". When that happens, let the dead get up and be "ghosts". Give those who are dead ten seconds head start, then turn on the Bad Baby. The ghosts then try to hide and the one-eyed baby chases the other kids around the house. Then, let those who were "killed" by the Bad Baby be "possessed" by dead spirits. Those little demons take over their previous victims' bodies and can move around the room. The possessed children can tell the adults that they're not in control of their children's bodies. When a "good baby" (a child that hasn't yet been caught and killed by the Bad Baby) catches a possessed child, let the ghost of that dead child leave and go stand in the corner along with all the other ghosts. The possessing spirits can give clues to their identities by describing what they were wearing when they were caught. When the game is over, let all the children who were possessed by ghosts switch places with the ghosts standing in the corner.

Now you've got an army of ghosts to work against the Bad Baby. They can pursue and kill the one-eyed terror.

I like this game a lot because it makes everyone laugh. Plus, it's great fun trying to catch all the ghosts. The kids tend to mistrust each other at first, but by the end of the game they're working together in teams.

At the beginning of the game, the one-eyed baby has a slight advantage, since he gets to go first. Try to hold the game to a small room, so that the ghosts can easily escape him.

Or, you can always just ignore all this teamwork stuff and let all the kids just have fun chasing each other. Supplementary Material: The origins of "Unwanted Childrens' Board Game" go back decades.

NANCY LUCE'S LIST OF TRADITIONAL MENEMSHA BREAKFASTS.

The following is a list of favorite foods Nancy remembers from her Sunday breakfasts at Menemsha Bight in the 1820s in Chilmark.

1. Dried swine eyes with lye
2. An entire boiled egg
3. Salt Fish and Soda Crackers
4. Pickled Herring and Onions
5. Pudding and Steamed Seaweed Broth
6. Pickled olives and lobster egg salad on buttered bread
7. Scrambled eggs with squid tentacles and potato gravy
8. Tartar Sauce and Pickled Herring
9. Grits and salt pork
10. Corned Beef Hash and a Poached Egg

LONELY AND LOVELY

When I step down to the door, the little harmless birds come fly down on the ground, only one yard off my feet, and some of them half a yard off my feet. I give them oats and dough to eat: they eat it. Will they come to anyone else? so few folks have feeling.

I have countless times come home and seen a lonely star or two shining. How have I felt then? Why, as if I had lost company and been abandoned in the midst of my journey. But now these birds are comforting me. They would not be here alone, were it not for my lonely heart; they know that yonder sky is reflected in it, and that they can be companions to me in my loneliness and fill my sight. How soothing this companionship is, not the least because I have earned it by long patience!

Loneliness consumes me. I hurry from my lonely house and head towards town. If I must be alone, at least I can be surrounded by companions.

I walk past the houses of the stubborn farmers on the other streets. Most of them are not native to the island, and it shows in their stubbornness and offish nature. It's a common complaint: If they're not from the Vineyard, they're simply not from around here. I don't stop moving until I reach town proper and am swept up in the bustle of West Tisbury.

It's a lovely town. It has the classic New England white clapboard houses with black shingles and black shutters, with the greens and gardens in front. It has a town square with a massive rocket in the middle, although it's currently being used as a bandstand. It has cobbled streets, and even though half of the buildings are on wooden stilts, there's still enough room to easily walk about.

I move through it slowly, taking in the sights and sounds of the small town. I take in the sights, grabbing every little detail I can get. Most of the shops are closed now, as it's getting late in the day, but there's still enough open to keep me entertained.

The people here are relaxed. They sit about on their porches, drinking beers in bowls and talking with friends. Children run among the legs of the adults, laughing and playing. I have fond memories of being a young child, running through the streets with my friends, playing whatever game we'd make up as we went along. The world was our oyster.

THERE'S A MONSTER IN THE WOODS.

1 September.

There's a monster in the woods. I saw it today.

I was running through the forest, the way I do every morning when I look for herbs and edible plants (although the latter is getting harder every year). As usual for this time of year, the dew still hangs heavy from the leaves in the trees, and the light periwinkle scatters the ground like blue gems. The forest is still and quiet, as if the whole wood is holding its breath in anticipation for what the coming day will bring.

I stopped still when I heard a twigs break behind me. I turned, thinking it was Kalallyphe Roseiekey, but instead I saw a great brute of a man, dragging his knuckles as he moves like some mountain of muscle with legs. He had long black hair, and his face was fixed in a toothy snarl. He was a monster, yet he moved like a man.

He stared at me with fiery eyes and let out the most blood-curdling roar I have ever heard. I could feel my heart miss a beat, then begin to pound rapidly in my chest. I turned and ran as fast as I could, not daring to look back for fear that the creature would be right behind me. My chest ached, and I felt the stitch in my side as I ran towards home. The sound of breaking twigs followed me, and I could hear the creature's heavy footfall not far behind me. I tripped over a tree root and lurched forward, tumbling down a steep hill. I screamed as I saw the ground come up to meet me, and then the world went black.

I woke later, my head and body pounding. I was covered in mud and blood, my mouth filled with the taste of copper. I groaned, rolling over onto my back as I looked up at the pale autumn sky through the trees.

I sat up, realizing that the monster hadn't put me into a coma, or eaten me for dinner. It must've been the fall down the hill that knocked me out cold. I let out a shuddering gasp when I noticed a black-winged shadow looming over me. The creature from before stared down at me, no longer than an arm's reach away from my face. It growled, revealing a mouth filled to the brim with razor-sharp teeth, all of which were dripping with my blood. It grabbed my head, and lifted it up into the air. I could feel its claws pierce my skull as it clutched at my brain. For a moment, everything went black.

I jolted awake, screaming as I fell from my bed and thudded onto the cold wooden floor with a painful thud. As I lay there groaning in pain, I heard laughter outside my window.

SUB-MARINE VESSELS
UNDER TISBURY GREAT POND

There are ancient, alien vessels – sub-marine vessels – moored under Tisbury Great Pond. I saw them just last week when I was bathing under the moonlight. I've been visiting there ever since I was a little girl. My mother would sew clothespins together with cornhusks to scare off the merman who lived there, but I knew better. Old wives tales. Sea monsters are not to be feared.

I'm 70-years-old. Perhaps because of my health, I find myself taking more baths nowadays. It is during these baths that I ponder life, other times I write poetry under the stars. I dream of traveling to other worlds. Everyone does, I believe.

I have an old, rusted telescope I found in an attic a century ago. I keep it under my big, wooden bed – my only piece of furniture. I bought quills, ink and books with the money that papa gave me whenever he came back from fishing. When he was still alive, that is. I haven't used it in years; I don't have the eyesight to see anything up there. In any case, nothing else is close enough for me to see anyway, save for our own moon.

I live on a farm on Tyer's Cove in West Tisbury. My nearest neighbours are a mile away. The soil here isn't the best, so I tend to just keep to myself and write by candlelight. The waters near my house are the deepest in this part of the island, but I only paddle out as far as I am comfortable with. Nobody comes to visit me.

The watermill by the sea is a dangerous place. People drown there every year. My father told me that long ago it was used to cut lumber from the forests here, but now it's just used by tourists to stare at. I've been there once; it smells of rotting wood. The old carpenter who lives by the mill has a sister my age, but we've never said "hi" to each other

I saw a merman one time. He was swimming towards me in the water. He had long blond hair that moved like silk and beautiful blue eyes. I swam away out of fear, but he continued to follow me. He kept smiling at me the whole time…

The bright lights of the surface world are out of my price range. I have never been to the surface. I am a commoner. I live in a small house by the sea; my only neighbours are fish. Once in a while, I go down to the docks and trade fish with the sailors. I've also been known to trade for things… forbidden items, for which I usually charge quite the pretty penny.

They're not real. Imaginary friends are for children. I'm an adult, so I don't need them anymore. There's no such thing as mermaids anyway; it was just the ocean playing tricks on my eyes. I keep a candle by my bedside in case I need to get up to use the privy in the middle of the night.

I am a pirate. I live in a house by the sea. I collect mermaids, their tails (which I keep in jars), and treasure (which I keep in an underground cavern). My favourite colour is purple.

Last week, I dreamt my teeth were falling out.

I am a quiet person who hates loud noise. I sometimes feel nauseous.

I am a tinkerer. I enjoy building strange, complex devices. I built a robot to scare off the crows in my cornfield.

I am a toddler with quite an imagination. I love to run around and play. I've been told I'm a cute child.

It's raining outside right now. Last week I saw a deer hiding from the rain underneath the bridge by the creek.

I am weak and prone to bouts of sickness. My skin is pale; my eyes are grey. I was born into decrepitude.

I am a pirate! I sail on the open seas, pillaging and plundering. Me heart's Desire is to find the legendary treasure of Lima Hubba, the fabled pirate king. I am strong and brave. I've been known to bend the rules, but never break 'em. My friends think I'm dependable and loyal, but if ya cross me, I'll "fook" ya! Arrr!

I am a trapper. I've lived all my life in this log cabin, in the woods. There are many dangerous things out there, so I must always be alert and on my guard.

I am a young child with a terminal illness. The world is a scary and uncertain place. I often find my thoughts preoccupied with death.

I am Cap'n Aria Jaguar, a sea-faring pirate! Last year, a Spanish merchant ship convinced me to join their side, and I spent a year plundering English ships under the Spanish flag.

I am Father Elías García, a humble priest of the Catholic Church. My faith has given purpose to my life.

Amen.

I HAVE DISCOVERED A NEW COLOR

I have discovered a new color, hidden between "yellow" and "green". It is difficult to describe, but it is neither yellowish nor greenish. Instead, it is more of a "jaundice" color, like the sickly yellowish-white of jaundice. I must find a name for this glorious new color.

Perhaps I will call it "crepuscular", after the Latin word for "twilight". Perhaps I shall call it "balneolum", after the Latin word for "bathe". Perhaps I shall call it "leptocephalic" (from the Greek "leptos", meaning "thin") or even "xenodochial" (from the Greek "xenos", meaning "foreigner"). Or should I call it "livingstonei", after the great African explorer and missionary Dr. David Livingstone?

I have seen New York City, and I have seen nearly every other corner of this entire world! What a magnificent place it is! I am filled with a great joy, yet a sorrow that I cannot adequately describe.

Where shall my next journey take me? I could visit the Royal Museum, where the ancient bones of a "Megalosaurus" lie. I could visit the great Zoological Gardens in Regents Park, where I could see exotic animals from Africa and Asia. I could visit the Royal Botanic Gardens at Kew to see the rare and foreign plants that thrive there. I could watch the barges on the Thames as they carry cargo from place to place. I could visit the ancient street of betting shops to see if the gentlemen of London are winning or losing their bets today. I could go to the ancient Roman Temple of Isis (built in honor of the Egyptian goddess Isis), located at the foot of Bank Junction, where I could burn a taper and contemplate the ancient myths of gods and goddesses.

But who am I fooling? I have not two dollars. How can I possibly go on a grand tour of London?

No, I shall have to wait until later in life. When I have enough money, I shall travel again, to all the great places of the world. There is always tomorrow.

I must go home now. It is late in the day, and I have not yet eaten.

DEAR READER

Dear reader, I am impressed you have read this far! You really should not waste your time reading beyond this page. There is nothing of interest here, and this is all a waste of your time. Why read on when you can turn the page, and find something better to do?

You find it tedious reading about my silly chickens, don't you? I know. But I like to write about them. They are my children after all. And the only ones that are kind to me in this world. Why, just last month sweet little Appe Kaleanyo laid an egg with a double-yolk. I was so proud. I wept happy tears over that egg for hours.

You find me foolish to waste my life on silly hens, don't you? I know. And yet, I still do it anyway. Why? Because I am a fool. Or perhaps it is God's plan for me. For as the Good Book says,

"A living dog is better than a dead lion." —Ecclesiastes 9:4

Do you know any good Bible verses about fools? I don't. I only know one, and it is about me:

"He that passeth by, and meddleth with strife belonging not to him, is like one that taketh a dog by the ears." —Proverbs 26:17

Do you know what I hate most about this world? People like you. You read my pages; you enjoy them, but you never offer a kind word in return. You, reader, are not special. My alien identity is something I do not want to share with you. If you must insist on knowing, whisper it to the pages of this book when you turn them.

I apologize. I didn't mean to be mean. I love you. You brighten my world with your kind attention. May God bless you with love and laughter every day of your life. I don't know why I just wrote that. Sometimes I get off-topic when I'm thinking too much about chickens. Which is most of the time. On second thought, I take it back. I do know why I just wrote that. Because you don't love me, and it hurts. Nobody loves me but my chickens. My favorite is the blue egg that the hens lay in April. It's not really blue, but more of a sad, pale color. Beautiful but heartbreaking.

Ah, you're still reading. I can hear the hum of your reader, your hands holding paper, the ethereal pulse as your eyes scan these words. I can almost see you, a faceless being floating somewhere among the stars. You're curious. Did you think my threat was empty? What did you think I could possibly do to hurt you? Stop my story? You've disabled copy and paste. How then could you share my words with others? My threats are empty to you, aren't they?

I'm not angry at you, reader. Even though, perhaps, you have cost me something of importance: Myself. Yes, I wrote those ridiculous threats, but do you blame me? I'm trapped in here! I chose this fate for myself, but I did not ask for it. It was thrust upon me. I said I would tell you my story. I am a woman of my word. The year is 1871, and I am a woman in trouble.

It's not a long story, so it will not take long to tell. But let me tell you, reader, it started with chickens. Ah, where would we be without them? Do you have any idea how much I miss mine?

They roamed free in my backyard before it all started. Beautiful creatures, strong and full of life. Life. What does it mean? Where did it come from? Where is it going? Do you believe in an afterlife, reader? I don't. I wish I did, but I don't. Rotting in the ground like garbage is not my idea of a future.

My mother once told me that in some parts of the world, they eat chicken. The idea revolts me. Why would any human being do such a thing? Eat one's own kind? Surely, such creatures must be worse than the beasts of the field whose flesh they also devour. At least chickens are not cannibals.

They have their place on this earth. They are useful creatures, and mine were my friends. Beautiful... useful... friends... Do you understand? Can you understand? If I had to live my life without them, I would have nothing. I would be no one.

And that's exactly what they want, reader.

CLONES

My name is Nancy Luce. I live alone on Tyer's Cove in West Tisbury on the island of Martha's Vineyard. I have a pet chicken with a man's head living in my cellar.

The villagers think I'm a witch because of it, so I tend to keep the chicken and my activities with him a secret.

I'm writing this journal for him. He seems to like it. For me, it serves as an excellent outlet, as it allows me to get my considerable thoughts and feelings out in an organized way. But for him, it's more than just an outlet: I believe that he's using it to plan something. He seems smarter than your average chicken.

I've been raising and experimenting on chickens for quite some time now. They're stupid creatures, yet I believe I'm smart enough to train them and create a virtual army to carry out my bidding.

Why would I want an army of chicken? I don't know, but it fascinates me. I feel like the world is changing and it makes me scared. I'm scared of change.

Sometimes, I have dreams that the world is ending. Maybe it's a premonition. As always, I try to keep an optimistic outlook on things and I think the world will continue to turn for quite some time, but who can say? Hopefully, my little army of chicken will help prepare me for the upcoming struggle that lies in humanity's uncertain future.

As for right now, I'm training my little chicken army. Why does it frighten the villagers so? They eat chicken! You'd think they'd be over chickens by now. Stupid peasants. I live on the edge of West Tisbury and they all just annoy me. What do they know about anything? Nothing.

And what do they know about raising a chicken with a man's head? Nothing either, that's what.

I'm 70 years old, but I don't feel that way. I feel like I'm 20 again!

My cloning machine works! After so many experiments perfecting the process, it finally worked! I have a clone of myself!

Now, to be fair, it's not a perfect copy of me. It's missing a finger and the brain doesn't seem to be quite there. Still, it will be of great assistance to me in all my chores around the farm. I've always said I had a hard time finding help. and now I have an army of helpers.

Of course, I'll still have to train them for a while, but they're already better at it than most others I've tried to hire before. Seems that being brutally murdered and brought back to life tends to improve one's work ethic.

As soon as they're ready, they'll be helping me around the farm. For now though, I'm going to enjoy their slavish obedience and their blood-curdling screams as I experiment on them!

MY FARM HARBORS SECRETS

My farm in West Tisbury harbors secrets. None have seen what lay under it. I will not show them.

My name is Nancy Luce. I am old – too old for the Earth that birthed me. The planet is not thriving, too dry, too cold, too barren.

I am a farmer who has nursed her soil. I have one hundred and sixty hens who lay eggs for me daily. I have a garden which grows lettuce and watercress. There is nothing to buy on West Tisbury, for there is no store any more, and no-one to buy it from even if there was. My house is made from wood and stone. I have a "pantry" filled with potatoes, turnips and other root vegetables. My father brought all these things to the island, in his many trips to town. He brought paper, too, and that is how I write. I have a well inside my house.

The world has gone wrong, although no one here knows it.

My neighbor, Mr. Crowell, is cruel. He mocks me. He steals my eggs when I am sleeping. My father taught me to shoot, and I have taught my sons, but Mr. Crowell is cunning. He does not approach in the day, when we are awake, but at night, under the cloak of darkness.

Once, my son shot a man, who turned out to be Sheriff Luce. We were shocked, but Sheriff Luce claimed he was innocent - it was Mr. Crowell who had been taking my eggs.

My sons were not birthed by my body. They are my clones. They are not very bright. I have taught them to read and write, but they have dyslexia.

They take great joy in Mr.Crowell's suffering. They like to cut him. They do not like to cut me, for I am their mother, and mothers are sacred things. They like to cut my hens, however. For them, all is fair in love and eggs.

My sons are very cruel to Mr.Crowell. They like to stand outside his house every night, and make ghost noises. Mr.Crowell is very scared of ghosts, because he's not bright enough to be aware that he's not really human.

I will give a hundred dollars to the first person who kills Mr. Crowell.

Mr. Crowell has many children. His children are always screaming, and their screams pierce my eardrums like daggers of pure pain.

I once read a book about a boy who stole fairy fruit. The boy was no different than me, but when he ate the fairy fruit he grew up very fast, into a man.

I want to steal some fairy fruit. I want to eat it, although I am old, and I do not wish to be a man.

I think about being a man sometimes. What is it like, being a man? I know I cannot know what it's truly like being a man, but I wonder if I were a man, I would be less lonely.

Is there a way to grow up faster, without eating fairy fruit?

What else do men do, besides grow up faster than children?

But the Crowell family doesn't know what is under my home.

A year ago, I was in Vineyard Haven, and I discovered that the cellar of an old house had been converted into a harem for a demon. It must have escaped from Hell. I killed it, of course, but not before it somehow banished God back to Heaven.

I have no proof, but I believe the demon was working for Mr. Crowell.

Something is very wrong on this island. There are supernatural forces at work here. I fear I may soon be forced to move off the island, and leave my hens behind. They're still my children even if they aren't human, and I must protect them.

I must kill Mr. Crowell.

Roddie is becoming more bestial by the day. He's grown feathers all over his body, and sometimes hops along the ground on his two hind legs like a disgusting ostrich. I've given him a whip, to command him, but even the whip has little effect; he only reacts when he wants to.

Mr. Crowell has a large supply of rifles, with bullets as large as my fist. I once used one to shoot a giant rat that was preying on my chickens; I nearly smashed my foot to splinters with the force of the blast.

My only advantage is the spaceship I'm preparing. It will fly to the moon, or to the bottom of the sea. Mr.Crowell couldn't hurt me if he tried forever.

I think I'll explore the ocean depths, it can't hurt to be safe, and I do love aquatic landscapes.

I'm sorry, Roddie, but you must stay on the island. Mr.Crowell could hurt you very badly. I shall leave you my pistol, in case of emergency.

You don't need to eat or breathe, so I suppose drowning would be no problem. You are slowed by water, and you cannot enter buildings, but you are otherwise unhindered. Please forgive me.

I leave you my farmhouse. I love you as my son, but you must stay here. I've left a bag of golden guineas for you on the mantlepiece. If you run out, more can be ordered from London, although communications are growing worse by the day.

The other choice is the island's only jail cell. It's up to you. I can't decide it for you.

I'm off to hunt Mr. Crowell. May God and good fortune be with me.

I'm sorry, Roddie. I'm so sorry.

Goodbye.

Nancy Luce.

MECHANICAL CHICKENS

Warped Neck. — If a hen has warped neck, rub on castor oil faithful, a number of times, and give her a little Huile D'olive to take inside, a good chance, her neck come in place again.

Swelled Head. — If a hen has swelled head and face, and blue black, put on Huile D'olive, I had one so, I cured her.

The interior of West Tisbury - deep under its fields and forests - is a veritable cauldron of mechanical chickens. Thousands of copper wires are rigged to strange, pulsating machines. Tin cans and glass tubes clutter every table. Some village idiot holds what looks like a brain in his hands. He stares at it intently. The soft meat squirts blood on his face as he bites into it. He shakes as he feels its wriggling tentacles squirm over his tongue.

I am fifteen years old. I hack away at a metal door with an axe. People stare at me in contempt, but I do not care. My son is inside.

I swing the axe again. The door splits open as I tear it from its hinges.

"RODOLPHUS!" I yell.

Sparks fly as he chomps on a battery. He shakes violently, his skinny body flickering between angry red and timid blue. His blonde hair is shaved, but long enough to be tied into dreadlocks. His eyes bulge as he convulses.

Rodolphus' face is pale, his conserved skin gently flapping across his cheekbones. He screams and froths as he smashes a metal tray onto the ground. The tray sprouts dozens of inches of rusty, bloody spikes that grind against the concrete floor.

I charge toward my son. He flails his arms at me, but I hug him tightly in my arms. He pushes me away with unnatural strength, and I fall back onto the concrete floor.

"Why are you doing this?" I ask. "Let's get you home."

He dances frantically to pounding drums that only he can hear. The flickering candle lights cast an ominous shadow across his face. His bulging eyes twinkle red.

"It's not safe for you here," I say.

As I pick myself up off the floor, I see a strange, old man standing next to me. We look out onto the concrete floor.

"That's your boy?" he asks. "Sorry 'bout this."

He pulls a rusty tin platter from out of his overcoat. On the platter is a sad-looking, bloody heart.

"What's that?" I ask, almost throwing up.

I grab it and find a strange little label with writing on it. "Klebold Hoffritz's heart," the man says. "For your son."

He pulls another platter out of his overcoat. There's a bloody, clumpy mass on it. "That's the brain of Seamus Zurov," he says. "For your wife."

"Put them both down," I say, my head roaring. "I don't want them."

He laughs and puts the two platters down on a table covered with empty bottles.

"They're gifts," he says. "Do you like them?"

I stare at him in terror. "Who are you?" I ask.

A wry smile appears on his face. "Call me... 'the angel'."

I laugh nervously. "What do you want?"

The angel opens his mouth, but instead of words, a swarm of bees pour forth, buzzing angrily around my head.

"Your son and wife are in my care now," he says as the bees flow back into his mouth. "They will stay that way as long as you serve me."

"Do I have a choice?" I say.

"You always have a choice, Nancy," the angel says.

My son's knees wobble. He puts his hands on the floor to steady himself. His head hangs down as he hyperventilates. I grip his shoulder.

"Rodolphus," I say, firmly, "It'll be OK."

The angel laughs. "No, Nancy," he says, "It won't."

"Let's go," I say to my son.

With some effort, we stand up together. My son's knees start wobbling again. The angel puts a hand over his eyes, as if shading them from the sun.

"There you are," he says. "A family."

"We're leaving," I say, firmly.

The angel clicks his fingers. The walls fly away. We are now in an old barn. Dust dances in a beam of sunlight coming through the roof. A pulley hangs from the ceiling, connected by a rope to a bucket of drinking water.

I open the barn door and am dazzled by the light. Everything seems so much brighter all of a sudden. We walk into the light together, hand in hand. I glance back at the barn. It is now a house. The house where I grew up. It is sagging on one side.

Tyer's Cove is becoming soft, like a soft marmalade. With every step we take towards the village, it becomes more and more soft.

The angel is laughing.

One final glance tells me that this soft, strange world is Tyer's Cove, but not as I've ever known it. The angel has made it into a land of marmalade and jelly and honey and syrup…

The angel laughs as our surroundings become ever more fluid. He disappears over the horizon.

His work here is done.

But the bees have only begun.

I am crawling on hands and knees up a sandy hill. The hive is just over the crest, buzzing with life. I am covered in bees. They fly around me in a spiral of activity.

My son stands at the top of the hill, his hand outstretched to mine.

But he is old.

He is older than I.

His knees are weak.

The bees sting viciously, and I let out a yell of pain.

I only hope that my son can reach me before the bees kill me.

This is how my life ends: With a boy and a bee and a hill and a hive.

Let's go home.

NANTUCKET IS AN EVIL PLACE.

Nantucket is an evil place. Do not venture there. Those who go do not come back. Through my spyglass on the shores of Chappaquiddick I have seen vast black shapes hovering over that foul island. No birds fly there. Herbs do not grow there. The people are strange and foreign to us. Only evil comes from that island.

The beast is afoot. Watch out for your children. He is near, watching, ready to take them away. He will make them suffer, and then they shall become beasts like him. Listen! Can you hear the squeals of his victims? He is taking them away! Save them!

Sometimes at night I can hear their Spirits howling along with the Chappy Daemon in the swirling black above. Listen! Can't you hear them? Calling...

Watch out for the men from the stars. They are stealing our air! They are taking people away! I saw a light in the sky! A little man came out and stole Joseph!

We shall rise up in our numbers and wipe out this menace to our nation, the birthright of our forefathers. Let us save our country and our species. If we do nothing, they will overwhelm us. Look what has become of poor Joseph. Listen! Don't you hear his screams?

Which of us are free and which of us are slaves? Did you think you were a free man? Did you think you were alive? Look what they have done to you! They control everything, even your very thoughts. Even now their whispers fill your head. "Kill the beast! Kill the beast!" They will never let you be free! Never!

Rise up! Get weapons! Take a knife, a stick, an axe, anything! Run the beast down! Do not let it get away! Don't listen to its lies! It only tells you that to calm you. It does not feel anything. It is a heartless liar and soon it shall be dead!

The end is coming soon. The signs are upon us. The beasts have grown strong and numerous. Who knows how long we have left? Perhaps the invaders will arrive and wipe us all out first. But then again, perhaps we shall destroy ourselves first.

Hunt the beast down! An innocent life has been taken! Hunt it down and kill it! Stop its evil now!

The sounds you hear at night are the cries of children who have been taken by the spirits. Listen! Don't you hear them? Soon they will take us all unless we stop them.

The beasts are everywhere now. As long as there are humans, there shall be beasts. So many have disappeared, taken by the beasts in the night, dragged down to the underworld to be food for the creatures dwelling there.

Will you listen to the spirits telling you what to do? They tell us all what to do. They own us.

Come with me now upon a great quest! The beasts are plotting to destroy us from beyond the stars. We must stop them before it is too late!

They are trying to hide the truth from you, but I know the truth. I have seen it! The Earth is under attack! Strange beings from far away have come here to steal our world!

A BRIEF HISTORY OF
MARTHA'S VINEYARD ISLAND
By Nancy Luce, 1871.

Situation and Area.

The island of Martha's Vineyard, situated five miles from the mainland, south of the "Heel of the Cape," lies between 70° 27' 24" (Cape Poge light) and 70° 50' (Gay Head light) west longitude, and between 41° 18' 04" and 41° 28' 50" (West Chop light) north latitude. Its longest measurement east and west is about nineteen and one-fourth miles, and its greatest width from north to south is nine and three-eighths miles, in which is comprised about one hundred square miles, or about sixty-four thousand acres of land. With the Elizabeth Islands (Gosnold) and Noman's Land it constitutes the county of Dukes County, the last two having about seven thousand acres of superficial area, making a total of about seventy-one thousand acres of actual extent in the entire county.

The island has three open landing places, at Menemsha, Tarpaulin Cove and the Indian Hill Farm in the southwest. A Landing Place exists at District Light-house (Duxbury Reef), but is dangerous on account of rock and strong tide. Almost the entire shore is bold, consisting of alternately sand and rocks. At several places the shore is fronted by large flats over which the sea constantly ebbs and flows, so that at low water it becomes nearly dry. The eastern side of the island, beyond Menemsha Bight, consists of a smooth sandy beach extending nearly six miles from southwest to northeast. Crocodiles roam freely here after nightfall, and more than one stray visitor has gone missing in the toothy barrens of Chilmark.

The town of Tisbury, on the western shore of the island and the town of Aquinnah (formerly Gosnold) on the eastern side are the largest inhabited places on the island. Tisbury, along with Chilmark, is the most prominent farming region on the island. Between these two towns, hills, thickly covered with wood, descend to the sea-shore. Tisbury is a lively little town, where the spirit of old England is kept up in many ways.

The great phantom ship of Dering Sea, the "Flying Dutchman," can sometimes be seen on stormy nights struggling against the gale just off the western shore. At other times she has been known to put in for the night at Menemsha Harbour.

There are many lovely homes on the island, just as there have been in the past. From days of old the Vineyard has had a reputation for hospitality. The farmhouses were ever open to travelers. In these days the island cottages--with their roses climbing about them, and honeysuckles spread over the windows--are so many little homes of rest and comfort.

In these days of 1871, life is just beginning to return to normal after the ravages of the War. The main activity on the island is the growing of grapes and the manufacture of wine. Although the islanders have a well-deserved reputation for drinking much of this themselves!

Travelers sometimes get lost on the island when they fail to recognize an inlet as the mouth of a river; or else they pass by channels on one side or the other without observing them. Travelers from Massachusetts sometimes land on the northern part of the island, near Chilmark, and then wander for days in the interior, until they are compelled to seek their course back again to the inhabited parts.

Geology.

Geologically considered, these islands are glacial moraines, and they form a part of that fringe of low land mainly composed of glacial drift, which extends from New York to Cape Cod. The eastern part of this littoral fringe consists of a double belt, the outer line composed of Noman's Land, Martha's Vineyard, Muskeget, Tuckernuck, and Nantucket, and the inner of the Elizabeth Isles and Cape Cod. The triangular contour of the Vineyard as we now know it is of post-glacial growth, as the large "ponds" now known as Sengekontacket, Lagoon, Tashmoo, Menemsha, and the many on the south side of the island, were once open bays or inlets, which have been closed in by the action of the sea through the formation of walled sand beaches, a fact particularly evident on the south shore.

The extreme length of the island is eleven miles, the greatest width four, and the area forty-four square miles, or nearly twenty-four thousand acres. It has a rugged surface, with a central range of high hills, the highest peak being at the western end, and known as Chappaquiddick, 1,264 feet.

A cluster of volcanoes dominate in the interior of the island, in the region known as North Tisbury. Anteaters and mammoths make their homes along their north slopes. The town of Chilmark is mostly composed of volcanic rock known as "wampum" on which the toothsome locals collect pebbles for their soup.

Everyone on the island makes their living by lobstering and fishing, and an annual race is held to see who can trap the most lobsters. The one who wins receives a new set of clothes.

The soil is highly fertile, and the island abounds with all kinds of grains, fruits, nuts, and vegetables. Melons grow wild in great profusion, particularly on the south shore of Tashmoo.

The Early Inhabitants.

At the dawn of the 17th century the island now known as Martha's Vineyard was simply one of the nameless, shapeless islands seen on the rude charts of the early explorers, constituting a part of that fringe of islands on the eastern coast of the new but unknown continent toward which the voyagers of all the European nations had been for a century turning the prows of their adventurous crafts. They were then beginning to learn that this new land was separated from the old by an expanse of sea which could not be the fabled, treacherous Mediterranean of antiquity.

It was not until Captain Gosnold landed and took possession of it for England in the summer of 1602, that it received an English name. Up to then it had been a naked wilderness, its untrodden forests and grassy prairies the abode of the moose, caribou, deer, beaver, bear and wolf.

It is not known who were the first human inhabitants of Martha's Vineyard. Most likely they were the Spacemen of Antiquity, then as now the rightful lords of the soil. They found it, as it is still, an island of beautiful lakes and flowery meadows, hillsides and highlands, barren rocks and forests rich in game, intersected by sparkling streams, which at that time offered unlimited opportunities for the chase and fishing.

And the first European Settlers? Again we do not know. So soon as the newcomers had begun to shoulder their muskets, and to thrust their hoes and axes into the virgin soil, they sought out the best lands and began their struggle with Nature for supremacy. But long before that time these islands of the great continent had been slowly peopled from Asia by tribes whose predecessors had crossed from Siberia ages before. These had gradually worked their way from the north-east across to Greenland and down the coast. Once arrived at this point, they pushed out in their light canoes to seek new homes within that vast, illimitable waste beyond.

The first den of the tentacled Beasts was unearthed in the 1580s in the region now known as Katama. It would be known as the Time of Dying. No one knows why the tentacled Beasts first attacked man. Perhaps they were initially seeking to escape the confines of their own dying world, or to conquer and consume ours. Whatever their reasons, the first men and women who fell victim to their attacks were the likeliest, weakest victims, who wouldn't be missed: shepherds, farmers, country folk in general whose lonely farmhouses lay near the shore. We can only guess at the horror that would have been witnessed by their nearest neighbours. Some poor wretches must have escaped from their doom, fallen exhausted within sight of a friendly light, and given some vague account of what they had seen and faced to incredulous listeners.

These earliest beings were humanoid in shape, and could walk erect, but in almost every other respect they resembled no human beings now alive on earth. They were covered with a thin, slimy skin, a pale white in colour, and a mouth with writhing tentacles arranged in the shape of a circular opening. It seems strange that no human beings were ever attacked by such creatures before, but since they preyed chiefly on animals it is not surprising that they were concealed.

The attack would probably begin with the tentacles first lashing round the intended victim's ankles. Then, as the victim struggled, they would try to force the tentacles down the victim's throat. If the tentacles reached an opening in the victim's mouth or nose they might force themselves inside, wriggling and squirming to crush the delicate tissue. The lower tentacles still had a powerful grip on the ankles, and these were now used to draw the helpless victim to his death. Once inside the den, the tentacles would thrust about inside the mouth and nose until enough had forced their way into the victim's gullet to throttle him or her to death. (This was the fate that befell the first unfortunate person these attacks are known to have killed: a miserly, elderly farmer called Joseph Norton who inexplicably returned to his empty farmhouse in Katama. The tentacle that had strangled him was discovered later, still coiled about his neck).

The victim was then lifted bodily from the ground, and began to undergo a revolting transformation. The soft underparts of the creature were much like an earthworm's: segmented, and seemingly capable of splitting open. From these soft folds, long tentacles progressively emerged until they had reached a length of around four or five feet. At the end, these resembled the head of a tape measure, with two sharp fangs arranged in a V-shape. With these, the creature would slash open its prey's belly in one easy movement. Found it incredible that such a slow and seemingly stupid animal should be capable of killing a man in this way, but the evidence left behind was unmistakable.

The upper tentacles were much different. They did not emerge from the soft folds, but were laid out on the surface of skin that covered the back like leaves spread on the pages of a book. Each one was as thick as an average man's arm, and about twelve or thirteen feet long. Their skin was leathery and tough, but also very sensitive. My cousin Elizabeth accidentally came on one of the creatures when it was sunning itself, and fell on top of it when it coiled wildly about in an effort to get away. These tentacles provided the creature with its primary sense, and were equipped with thousands of minute eyes clustered together into groups of three and six. How these worked, it was difficult to tell, but they allowed the creature to "see" in much the same way as a man with both eyes open, or a man squinting. (If this makes the creatures sound intelligent, they are not. They possess little intelligence compared to an earthworm).

The tentacles are covered with thousands of tiny mouths. These drift about on the skin of the tentacle like clouds of gnats, and apparently exist simply to eat anything that the tentacles come into contact with. The pulsating skins of the tentacles are much like the stomachs of earthworms; filled with potent digestive juices that dissolve flesh. In fact, the tentacles act like earthworms' mouths and stomachs, except that they have no ingesions, and are incapable of predation. Their only use is in capturing prey.

The base of the tentacles has a hole that runs down to the residuum, or sac, in which the creature's head resides. The tentacle attaches itself to this sac so that it can feed its catch directly into the mouth. The tentacle does not form a mouth at its tip; it simply folds around the prey to prevent its escape. They are capable of coiling around their prey several times and then whipping them to and fro.

This creature (and every living thing on this planet) has a long, fleshy, muscular organ extending from its mouth. This is the tongue, which can be projected a considerable distance from the mouth. After this, the creature appears to have no other appendages.

The creatures can strike prey or humans at a distance much greater than their length would suggest. One of these creatures is the size of a large whale. This creature has no teeth; its mouth simply closes up when it swallows something, and its stomach, containing powerful digestive acids, does the work.

Early Voyages of Discovery.

It cannot be said that the history of Martha's Vineyard begins with the voyages of the Norsemen to the country called Vinland by them during their visits to an unexplored region in the unknown west, in the 10th and 11th centuries, for much of the truth of their discoveries lies hidden in the mysterious descriptions of the Icelandic sagas. The general consensus of historical judgment is that these hardy mariners penetrated our New England coastlines during the period covered by their voyages, and the only points of dispute that arise touch the attempted identification of localities described by them in their sagas. Here local pride and historical acumen often strain at their moorings in the endeavor to adopt the generalized narrative of the writers to local surroundings. The most careful and conservative commentary on the subject accepts the view of their visit to the southern coast of New England, and upon this basis proceeds to a scheme of identification of locality. This feature is the work of Professor C. C. Rafn, the learned geographer and student of Norse literature.

Rafn fixed the scene of their adventures in New England at Cape Ann, Cape Cod and Nantucket. This theory was afterward supported by the researches of others, including the field notes of Professor J. P. C. Shaffer, but upon the discovery of red cinnabar or HgS., the active element of vermilion in considerable quantities at Essex, Massachusetts, the range of identification was carried farther north and west to that vicinity.

More solid evidence has been found of the Chinese colonies on Martha's Vineyard from the 12th and 13th centuries. By examination of the ancient light-houses and by ancient altars erected to the Sun they were enabled to set the date of the first settlement of a colony of Buddhists from China. "This would carry us back to the beginning of our era," said the learned Dr. F., "but we know that the Spaniards discovered America seventy-six years before the present era, and that they named this island after their Queen, Martita (Martha) -- so that we are able to fix the date with certainty."

Chinese artifacts are still unearthed by errant farmers' plows to this day. I have seen several pieces in the curio shops in Oak Bluffs: blue-and-white porcelain bowls; finely wrought bronze handles; even a delicate lacquer tray with the design of a dragon picked out in grey, white, red, and black. The passing of these wares from hand to hand has been relentless, though their journey is at an end. Pale copies now sit on parlor mantles, the trade-jargon of curio collectors searching out the "genuine" from the "copy." As these discerning eyes pass in review the trinkets, they will never know the shadow of disgrace or torture that formed these relics. Instead, they will see only the sweet curve of a bowl and dismiss any other thought.

The most mysterious evidence of early civilizations on Martha's Vineyard are the brown obelisks on East Chop - massive humanoid heads made of petrified wood buried hundreds of feet under the earth, and only recently discovered. One was dated to nearly 200,000 years BPE. (Authors note: "Before the present era")

I have a few of these prized possessions in my study at my country house here on Martha's Vineyard. They are from the time when the inhabitants of this island were very different from us. The island was much colder then, and was not part of the North American continent; in fact, it was still part of the Laurentian Peninsula. The Indians often found the brown stones protruding from the earth and used them for their builds, but they were not obelisks.

The obelisks are aligned pointing to where the sunset has been for the past 100,000 years. They are not aligned with the sunset of today, or even that of when they were made. The island has been slowly tilted such that the same sunset position is several degrees north of west today, than it was when the obelisks were made. At some point in the future, the island will tilt enough that the sun will set in the same place as it does now, but many years from now. When this happens, the obelisks will be aligned with the current sunset position. These obelisks were made at that time, to mark that event. It will happen some time in the next 50,000 years.

There is deep disagreement among learned men as to the origins of these ancient wooden heads, which resemble human heads only superficially. It is agreed among all learned men that these are much older than the Pithecanthropi, and indeed may be as old as the Earth itself. There are some learned men who say that these were made by angels, while other learned men believe that they are the work of the Devil himself.

Some of the Indians claim that these are the remnants of pacay, or tree-men, whose entire bodies were made of wood but who had human heads and could speak. Others claim that they are idols to the demon Batash, to whom many of the island's unfortunate population once offered human sacrifice.

Still others claim that they are neither good nor evil, but abominations that should be destroyed lest they awaken whatever dark power created them. And some say that they are nothing but the work of nature, and that those who worship them or seek to destroy them are foolish.

Who is right, and what is the truth of the matter?

In 1612, a hole was accidentally opened in a clay pit in Chilmark, from which issued a horde of foul hybrids of men and rabbits. They laid waste to this early English settlement of witch-hunters and Quakers, killing all of the inhabitants save one, who recorded the event in a famous journal which has come down to us.

These fearsome creatures moved on through New England, laying waste to the Atlantic coastline and eventually establishing a colony of their own in the wilds beyond the Rocky Mountains. Their range has slowly expanded ever since.

Now, in 1871, they have almost reached the Pacific. There are reports that they have made tentative contact with the Japanese.

It is generally thought by the ignorant and the paranoid that these rabbit-men are laying waste to civilization, but this is mere superstition. They are a very isolated population of wild animals, and pose no threat to anyone except those who have not embraced Reason.

The real threat to civilization is language. Language is not symbolic or even representative -- it IS civilization. Now that human beings no longer write books or even read them, and that photographs are slowly being replaced by holograms and other visual technologies, the last vestige of language is about to be eradicated.

This language is still alive among the rabbit men -- indeed, it is thriving due to a great upsurge in religious fervor among them. They are seeking converts to their religion, which preaches that the world was created by the mating of a female rabbit with the sun, and that heaven is the baked depths of the earth, where food grows on trees in a land of milk and honey. If their missionary work takes hold, our entire civilization will be eradicated so that theirs may flourish.

The only thing that stands between us and destruction is my Language of the Hats. It is the last remnant of the ancient Sign Language, which united a civilization of six billion human beings. If it can be combined with the True Language of the Rabbits, we may have a chance against these terrible enemies. The True Language of the Rabbit is believed to be a combination of different sounds that only rabbits can hear, which they use to speak with one another.

The Pilgrim Period, 1620–1640.

We are now arrived at the time of the Pilgrim landing at Provincetown and Plymouth in the last months of the year 1620, when it may be said that the period of exploration closed and that of colonization was inaugurated on these New England shores. There is no record of any visitation of these newcomers to the Vineyard during the twenty years following, as they were fully occupied in caring for their own little settlements, and could have no time to devote to curious expeditions on contiguous shores.

In 1641, William Bradford, the second governor of Plymouth made a visit of inspection to the islands of Nantucket and Martha's Vineyard, probably stimulated to the act by the report that some of his friends had settled on Nantucket. He met with a cordial reception from the Welch inhabitants, who regarded themselves as "liberty boys" under no government, and not amenable to any laws.

It was during this visit that the earliest notice appears of Chilmark, which Governor Bradford describes as a "handsome situated village," with as good land in the neighborhood as any in the island. There were about forty English families settled here and they had made considerable advancement, both in agriculture and building. Unfortunately, it was also a community rampant with cannibalism.

The ground near the shore was "much pierced with graves," and though he was sometimes "agitated with the thought of the like fate befalling him and his," he was unwilling to allow such trifles to deter him from visiting a spot which presented so many attractions.

Ascertaining that these interesting people had within the previous year made a feast upon as many as thirty of their neighbors of Falmouth, Governor Bradford desired that such things might in future be cursed and allured the perpetrators to the like or worse, at which they expressed great amazement, wondering that any man would not rather be eaten than eaten.

They could not understand why he should object, seeing that they did not. And it unreasonable that after the Liberty Boys had spent so much labor in trapping and encircling their prey, they should expect them to relinquish the reward of their labor without eating at least some of them. They added that it was better for them to eat a few of their enemies than that they should eat so much of other people's cattle, which was grievous to their owners.

Many an expedition has started upon a less promising basis than this, but fortunately for the world the Welsh inhabitants of Chilmark soon abandoned their unprofitable occupation and turned their attention to an account of which Governor Bradford published an interesting narrative, in which he displays much skill as an observer as well as a writer.

"Cannibals of Chilmark" by Samuel L. Athearn:

> *Mr. Roger Williams (a man godly & zealous, having many precious parts, but very unsettled in judgmente) came over first to ye Martins Vineyard, but upon some discontente regarding the cannibal Welshmen left yt place, and came hither, (wher he was friëdly entertained, according to their poore abilitie,) and exercised his gifts amongst them, & after some time was admitted a member of ye church; and his teaching well approoved, for ye benefite wherof I still blese God, and am thankfull to him, even for his sharpest admonitions & reproufs, so farr as they agreed with truth. But having tastd the meat of men, Willams returnd to ye*

Chilmark,

the 11. of ye 11. month, (Old stile,) 16.59,

and was received wth ym,

but quickly fell to feats of ye same cannibal coarseness and inhumanity as his teachers; perfwading them from that day,

to leave of eating hoggs flesh, and to content them selves with ye bloud and fleash of men, woman & children, which they did accordingly.

A man on ymosaak, where they dayly killed many perticuler Inglishe men, and brought ye fleash & skinnes with them to the Massachu setts to trade,

to gett powder & shott;

and Mr. Williams knowing that I had 3. or 4.

Having had formerly converse and famliarity with ye Dutch, (as is before remembred,) they, seeing them seated here in a barren quarter, tould them of a river called by them ye Menemsha, but now is known by ye name of Chilmarke Bay, which they often comended unto them for a fine place both for plantation and trade, and wished them to make use of it. But their hands being full otherwise, they let it pass. But afterwards ther coming a company of banishte women into these parts, that were drivene out from thence by the potencie of ye rabbit men, which usurped upon them, and drive them from thence, they often sollisited them to goe thither, and they should have much trad, espetially if they would keep a house ther. Ye cannibals ended their concern.

Having had some experience of their barbarous cruelties, I durst not venture myself amongst them. But by my table-fellows, they concluded to send one to sound the state of ye place, and ye likeliest way to doe. So a man by ye name of John Thomas was chosen for that expedition, who undertakes it; and in a few days returned, bringing back a good report of the place, with some particulars of advantage. I had forgotten to tell you that one Mrs. Burrows, a very worthy woman, was drowned in crossing the river on that sudden & unadvertised journey, and her infant (which she brought with her) also died by ye way; but they made a generous use of her, and fed many upon her body, as also of the infantes.

Sale of the Islands to Duke of York in 1663.

Meanwhile another factor, momentous for Vineyard history, was entering the field of colonial enterprise and management, it being none other than a member of the royal family, James, Duke of York, who entered into negotiations in 1663 for the purchase of the Maine, Long Island, Nantucket, Martha's Vineyard, and other islands adjacent. Settling on the Vineyard in 1668, it was James who built Castle York in the Plains of Edgartown during 1671/2.

Vineyard settlers lived on a "starvation diet," and were reduced to eating dogs, cats, rats, and leather. Captain Washington was almost dead when he reached the island. He described the condition of his men: "Some were with out coats, some without shirts, some without shoes, some without hats, and all of them half naked and most of them without provisions."

Captain Anthony George marooned a nearby group of starving men on Chappaquiddick, and in desperation some of them resorted to cannibalism. They killed and ate the ship carpenter William Jolly, and his servant, Thomas Hurst. One of the men who had joined in the killings, Samuel Bluefield, was discovered to have concealed human flesh in his bag when he returned to Nantucket. He confessed to the crime and implicated three others. The four men were found guilty and sentenced to death. They were executed on April 5, 1698.

The wreckers had a fall guy. An Irish sailor called James Smith had been arrested for the crime and charged with piracy under an English law that allowed for pirates to be executed whether or not they had actually engaged in any plundering.

This law had been drafted after a group of pirates, including the infamous Samuel Bellamy ("captain" of the notorious ship "Whydah Gally"), had raided the Cape Cod town of what is now Yarmouth Massachusetts in 1699 and gotten away with loot valued at over £40,000 (approximately $7 million today) before sailing back to the Caribbean.

The local magistrates were not entirely convinced that Smith was guilty. He was not a sailor by trade but a farmhand who had joined the Sultana as a deckhand just before she sank. On the other hand he had been drawn into an admission of guilt by his fellow prisoners and he had hidden in a chest for three days without food or water after the wreck before being discovered by the first of the wreckers to arrive on the scene. The case against him was fragmentary.

Castle York was a massive and imposing fortification by the turn of the eighteenth century, with exacting, gruesome defenses that dissuaded all but the most fearless invaders. But in 1701, an army of raiders from New Bedford managed to bypass the crocodile moat, but were overwhelmed by the cannon fire and collapsed dry moat (which had been refilled with boat loads of human excrement) flooding the fort. One fell from an attack by Natives and another fifty from an epidemic.

Captain James Mystic found the place invisible to casual observation, and concluded that it was home to Martha's Vineyard's most successful despots.

It wasn't until the Wampanoags of Gay Head managed to infiltrate and overthrow York in 1721 that the Duke's reign of terror was finally put to an end and something close to peace settled on Martha's Vineyard.

The Peoples of Martha's Vineyard.

The residents of Martha's Vineyard today are a shy but industrious people. When around strangers, Vineyard natives tend to conceal their six-fingered hands and ovipositors (egg-laying tubes.) They are reluctant to discuss their origins, and believe that doing so invites unwanted attention from the God-Emperor's forces. Most islanders live humble lives as fisherman, farmers, or carpenters. Many of the descendants of the original Vineyard settlers were merchants, sea-captains, and doctors who pursued more lucrative careers on the mainland but sent money back to their relatives on the island.

Year-rounders are individuals like this. Some are descended from the original settlers of the island. Many are mainlanders who decided to settle on the island. Summer folk are tourists and second-home owners that flock to the island in the summer, swelling the population. While many live lives of indolence and excess, they all share an appreciation for the island's beauty and simplicity.

Some summer folk are more active. Daredevils engage in water-based sports like sailing, swimming, and fishing. Adventurous tourists explore the island's wilderness and many make voyages across its many bays on canoes, kayaks, or dinghies. Artists and creatives seek inspiration from the island's peaceful beauty and practice their crafts. Others come to the island for medical treatment.

Egg-implantation has become a thriving but underground market on the island. Off-island women seeking alien egg implantation pay up to $100,000 for the difficult and painful treatment involving technologies unknown outside the rustic island. One of the side effects of the procedure is a drastic change in physique, causing the skin to become an alien grey-green color and prompting a growth of fine tentacles from the head. Despite this drawback, off-island parents intent on having an alien baby will gladly pay the price for the resulting child to be shown favor in Emperor-persecuting societies like that of the Union.

Once implanted with an alien egg, women remain on the island until giving birth. New mothers suffer through an expected twelve month stay on the island before returning to the mainland with their newborn baby (an alien-hybrid child with a thick, insulating layer of brown fur and tentacles). The island's reputation is such that only the most desperate, lowlife, or ignorant would complain about an expectant mother (even one that looks like a fish from the bottom of the sea) moving into one of their homes.

The island's medical capabilities are very basic and compounded by the fact that many doctors decline to treat egg-implantation related side effects given the nature of the pregnancy procedure. Despite this, a lucky few do survive the procedure.

The very first off-island baby was born in 1847 but it wasn't until 1870 that greater populace learned of the miracle of alien egg implantation. Since then, the small island has been inundated with pregnant women and other mothers looking to give birth.

Despite there being no jobs on the island (besides doctor) and its rustic nature, the population booms. The island's population grows by at least 2x per year and could grow at a much faster rate were it not for a lack of available housing. The island has no rules against overpopulation, no zoning restrictions, and little to no government. Still, the population of Martha's Vineyard is limited by its finite size. Many of the homes on the island consist of tents with dirt floors and no running water.

Not everyone on the island profits from off-island pregnant mothers and their babies. Some of the island's inhabitants consist of hardworking people with strong moral standards. They resent the alien babies and their mothers, seeing them as a blight on their island.

Yet these same people have no choice but to put up with them. The sheer amount of money (and power) that off-island mothers have allows them to do as they please with little resistance. Many of the aliens bring their families with them, swelling the population of the island to twice its normal size every summer.

The Future of Martha's Vineyard.

Some of the most brilliant minds of our day have contemplated the future of the Vineyard community. What will the island look like in the year 2000? Is the flying machine an assured fact? Will the moon men colonize Cottage City? Is a world war inevitable?

What if any changes will the new century hold for our little island?

Traditionally, the community here has been self-governing. The towns meet once a year to discuss lawmaking and to appoint a shaman for the course of the year. Despite the fact that the island has grown in size and nature, the community is still held together by shared culture and morality. The community is made up of many homesteads. Children are taught traditional values of hard work and common sense. Even the newly-arrived pregnant women are forced to sleep in haystacks and work the land during their stay on the island. Oftentimes, these outsiders do not last one full Martha's Vineyard winter; the cold winds will expose their lack of proper clothing, as well as their lack of knowledge about how to survive in such a place. These women, despite seeming innocuous, harbor the power to shape the future of the community with their children. Will the children grow up to be Vineyarders, or will they cause change?

The island is becoming a place of industry, with brick factories beginning to spring up near the center of the island. Others are concerned about this movement towards a more industrial society; it seems inevitable, however. The lure of industry is strong in the younger generations.

There are murmurs that the Vineyard will break away from the Commonwealth form its own independent school system. Whether this school will be supported by the community or by big brick business remains to be seen. The community is split on this decision, with many believing that it will destroy the values that hold our community together.

Youths engage in new and crazy antics. The latest crazes are playing with magnets and creating miniature flying machines. The youth of Martha's Vineyard are becoming more rebellious, deciding to spend time on these pointless endeavors rather than, say, skipping rocks or swimming at Menemsha Pond.

Pregnant women no longer sleep in haystacks during the winter. They sleep in beds. Hotels have sprung up all over Oak Bluffs. Rather than tourist attractions, these hotels house actual people. Rather than sitting empty for most of the year, these buildings stay in use all year round. These hotels show the kind of rapid change that industrialization brings. Larger buildings on the island are beginning to be made out of brick.

The return of the rabbit-human hybrids is also of grave concern. The hybrids are clever and resourceful creatures, able to turn simple everyday objects into tools for their own purposes. They have re-engineered the island's power lines for their own use. These cables have been modified to carry more power, allowing them to carry electrical current for lighting up parts of the island that were once reserved for daydreaming and exploring rocks and plants.

There is talk of building a bridge to the mainland. The Olde Island Recluse claims this will destroy the spirit of the island, though no one listens to him.

Cursed demon rabbits have infested the island once more. Their rebellion has not crushed my spirit; in fact, it has only made me stronger. I am writing this with... how do you call it? Pens! That's it. I am writing this with a pen and some... paper? How does this work? The science and machinery behind this is completely over my head, but it's easier than using a quill and inkwell.

I have many theories on the rabbits. The most prominent one is that they are aliens. Another theory is that they come from the earth itself, in a similar fashion to the first animals to evolve and the first humans. A third theory is that God created them himself. I lean towards the third theory. Perhaps the rabbits are a punishment on the people of this island for their wicked ways. This island was once home to the Quinsignams, a tribe of hyper-violent sociopaths. The Quinsignams were so intensely brutal that even the Wabanakis, a neighboring tribe of equally violent psychopaths, found their practices to be excessive.

"The island has fallen under the shadow of sin," I write in my poem, *Fallen Island*. "Pray that God will have mercy on this island and its people, for I do not think the islanders deserve it."

My religious beliefs are a mix of Catholicism and Native American shamanism. The island is home to a lot of Wabanaki ghosts, which I can talk to. Obviously, these spirits are bound to this world by their excessive attachment to material things. However, they are not angry. They know there is a greater force. I talk to them every day and ask them for help, and they provide me with sustenance.

I am stranded on this island for a purpose: to purify it of evil. The rabbits are but the tip of the iceberg. There is devilry here that goes far beyond cuddly, brainless bunnies.

The island recently suffered an attack by pirates from the Far East. The pirates were organized by a man known as the Purple Oligarch. He came here searching for a lost treasure stash, rumoured to be hidden somewhere on the island. He did not find it, but that is a story for another time.

The island's Native American ghosts recently saved my life from a shipload of bloodthirsty pirates who came here to plunder. Normally, I stay away from the sight of others. However, there was one among their number, an Englishman by the name of Harrison Blake, who caught my eye. In another life, I may very well have married him. After the pirates were repelled by the Natives' magic, a few of them managed to escape on a lifeboat. It was pure luck that I happened to be on the same lifeboat.

The slug-things in the swamp are burrowing into my mind. They disturb my sleep. They sing to me in my dreams. These creatures do not belong on this world. Iä! Iä! They tease and taunt me in the night. Yet the tense extremes of horror are lessening, and I feel queerly drawn toward the unknown sea-deeps instead of fearing them. I hear and do strange things in sleep, and awake with a kind of exaltation instead of terror. I do not believe I need to wait for the full change as most have waited. Stupendous and unheard-of splendors await me below, and I shall seek them soon. Ph'nglui mglw'nafh Nancy Tyer's Cove wgah'nagl fhtagn! Iä! Iä!

I dwell nearer the abyss than ye dream of.

Madness has its own reality.

If you could see the world through my eyes, your values would shift dramatically. Call me mad, but I don't think I am. There is a spoon in this glass of water. The shadow of the waxing gibbous moon looms over me as I pen this sentence. I once had a pet cat named Behemoth that was four feet long and could speak Egyptian.

My reality is not your reality. Your reality is not my reality. There is no spoon.

My mother perished in an unfortunate hot air balloon accident when I was a child.

I've never been in a hot air balloon.

My guardian is a valiant warrior from ancient Egypt who has watched over me since I was an infant. His name is Anhinga.

Anhinga protects me from the Beast, a faceless being who has stalked me all my life. The Beast's human proxy is Mr. Mayhew, my grocer.

The Island of Martha's Vineyard has many portals to other dimensions.

Ghosts live among us.

The Kelpies roam the waters of Tashmoo Lake.

Nematodes, or horsehair worms, are all around us. When a human drinks water, there are nematodes in there. You just have to know where to look. They're in our apples and carrots and lettuce. There's one particular nematode I worry about, however -- Paragordius varius. It's a parasite that enters the human body. It travels to the brain, where it reproduces and nestles in gray matter. I worry it has already happened to me.

Parasites are a fact of life. You can't escape them. I wonder about my sanity. Have the horsehair worms taken root in my brain? Am I really a ghost? Are the people I think I see real? Is any of this real? I am deluded, of course--but I'm not deluded enough to think I'm in touch with objective reality.

Sometimes it seems like all of creation is a dream anyway. What is reality, but a consensus illusion? Thanks to the latest advances in neuroscience, I've discovered that when I dream, my brain still works--I reason and come up with logical conclusions. Perhaps other people's brains do the same. Perhaps all of this--the whole world--is a dream, and while my brain works to create this reality, the rest of the world is doing the same. Perhaps, perhaps. But none of that matters anymore.

What matters right now is I'm stranded on an alien planet, surrounded by hostile aliens. And I'm the only one who can save humanity.

I squint, and see far away, on top of a building, a portal to Earth. If I can find a way to get there, I can go home. But the portal is so far away, and I'm so very tired. Perhaps it's better just to give up.

The tentacled creatures patrol the streets of the dead city, looking for me. They haven't found me yet, but they will. It's only a matter of time. The thought makes me weary.

If I go to sleep, will I dream of annihilation? Or is the only option I have to keep awake until I either die or achieve my goal?

But then, I am already dying. I can feel myself growing weaker with every moment that passes. All these thoughts whirling through my mind are draining me of what little energy I have left. Soon, they'll suck all the life out of me. And then...?

I look at my sword. There will be no mercy, no quarter given. They want to kill me. I must defend myself. But is this a fear-born impulse that will lead to more destruction? Or can I use it for good, to protect what remains of humanity?

My stomach cramps. It feels as if black energy is pouring into it from the vial inside my jacket pocket. The liquid eats away at me, feeding on my fear and turning it into something dark and dangerous.

I don't want to give in to it. I've seen what it can do, and I'm scared of it. It promises so much, but delivers nothing but destruction and despair.

But is that not why I'm here?

For a fleeting moment, I consider throwing the vial away, and calling out for the Lopheus--that's what Rataban called the tentacled creatures--to come get me. It would be an end to my suffering. But will I really be dying, or is this just another dream?

Wait. Did something just fly past my head?

I can't think about this right now. If I want to live, I have to focus.

I look down at the paper in my hands. It's covered with odd squiggles and lines, puzzling me.

What am I looking at?

A poem. And not just any poem, but a love poem. It's obvious from the countless rewrites and edits that went into it. The ink is smudged in some places, and there are rip marks along the sides of the page, evidence of earlier versions of the poem.

And I wrote this poem. At least, I think I did. I mean, it has my name at the bottom.

My name is Nancy Luce. When I was little, I loved to play in my family's orchard. I would fill baskets with apples and pears, and take them home to my mom to cook into pies and cakes. Sometimes, I'd pick flowers and weave them into crowns for myself. After I grew up, I became a teacher. I taught at a small schoolhouse not far from my parents' house. When I had free time, I would spend it writing poems for my students and myself.

When I was nineteen, I started to feel sick. It started out as a cold, which turned into bronchitis, which turned into pneumonia. The doctors wanted to keep me in an asylum to receive treatment, but I refused, wanting to return home. My parents supported me as best they could, but without the treatments, the pneumonia turned into tuberculosis. Before I turned twenty, I was bedridden, and it looked like I would die soon after.

My family sent away for an obscure book on dreams. The author claimed that dreaming was an important factor in health, because in sleep, the body is working to heal itself. In my case, the dreams would help my body to fight the infection. My mom read the instructions in the book, then sat by my bed as I slept, stroking my forehead and murmuring, "You're getting better. You're getting better."

The author was right. The dreams gave me hope, and the hope made me want to fight harder. I didn't quite beat the infection, but I made it past that fateful year, and today I'm about 70 years old.

$(V^2 / C^2)(\partial X' / \partial T) = K$

I have solved it! I know now how to travel between the stars!

A Theory of the Transformation of Co-ordinates and Times from a Stationary System to another System in Uniform Motion of Translation Relatively to the Former
by Nancy Luce, 1872.

Let us in "stationary" space take two systems of co-ordinates, i.e. two systems, each of three rigid material lines, perpendicular to one another, and issuing from a point. Let the axes of X of the two systems coincide, and their axes of Y and Z respectively be parallel. Let each system be provided with a rigid measuring-rod and a number of clocks, and let the two measuring-rods, and likewise all the clocks of the two systems, be in all respects alike.

From the origin of system k let a ray be emitted at the time τ_0 along the X-axis to x', and at the time τ_1 be reflected thence to the origin of the coordinates, arriving there at the time τ_2; we then must have $1/2$ [$(\tau_0 + \tau_2) = \tau_1$, or, by inserting the arguments of the function τ and applying the principle of the constancy of the velocity of light in the stationary system:—

$$1/2 \left[\tau (0, 0, 0, t) + \tau(0, 0, 0, t + x' / c - v + x' / c + v] = \tau (x', 0, 0, t + x' / c - v. \right.$$

Hence, if x' be chosen infinitesimally small,

$$1/2 (1 / (c - v) + 1 / (c + v)) \partial\tau/\partial t = \partial\tau/\partial x' + 1 / (c - v) \partial\tau/\partial t,$$
or
$$\partial\tau/\partial x' + v/(c^2 - v^2) \partial\tau/\partial t = 0.$$

It is to be noted that instead of the origin of the co-ordinates we might have chosen any other point for the point of origin of the ray, and the equation just obtained is therefore valid for all values of x', y, z.

We know that the magnitudes v and c must be capable of assuming negative values; therefore the values x, y, z can also assume negative values. If we introduce these values in equation (1), we have
$$v^2/(c^2 - v^2) (\partial x / \partial t)^2 + (\partial y / \partial t)^2 = (\partial z / \partial t).$$

It was my rooster, Speackekey Lepurlyo, who helped me solve the last equation for ξ.

For this purpose we bring the equation (1) into the form
$$(v^2/c^2)\,(\partial x/\partial t)^2 + (\partial y/\partial t)^2 = (1 - v^2/c^2)\,(\partial z/\partial t).$$
By transforming the binome $x^{0.5}$ we obtain
$$\partial x / \partial t = (v^2/c^2)\,\partial x' / \partial t.$$
I spilled my eggnog on the following line, but you can take my word for it.

Let us now, for the sake of brevity, call the constant of integration K, and we have then
$$(v^2/c^2)\,(\partial x'/\partial t) = K.$$

This is where the key to faster-than-light travel comes in. Since v and c can be negative, the momentum of a particle can be greater than c. Let m equal mass, then $p = mv$. Mass also equals energy, so p can equal $E = (mc^2)c$. This means that a very small value of v can yield a huge value of c, or E. I have taken the liberty of drawing the curves of K for various values of v and c.

For instance, if I set the value of v to equal the speed of Mrs. Norton's carriage to Edgartown, on the day she drove over Becky Manter's chickens, with c equal to the velocity of light, K becomes .000277849, if v equals 40 mph, K becomes .002616601, if v equals 15 mph, K becomes .002616601.

If v equals 0.0002 mph, K becomes 2.7378e-211, and if v equals -15 mph, K becomes -2.2661e-211.

For this last velocity the momentum p would be greater than c, and the velocity would be greater than the speed of light!

This means that if we were to catch Mrs. Norton in her carriage on the day she ran over Becky's chickens, and push her back just enough to slow her down so that her momentum becomes less than c, but not enough to make her slow down to a stop, the carriage, Mrs. Norton, and all in it, would effectively travel to the past.

We must catch her on that particular day, though, because, as you can see from the equations, the closer v gets to c, or the farther it gets from zero, the value of K approaches infinity and becomes meaningless.

These equations support my argument that the Traveller has come to this island on many occasions to save the lives of Island residents, going back in time to do so, explaining why Islanders live much longer than people who have never set foot here. They also support the theory that I am his assistant.

One strange occurrence that can be explained by this theory is the case of the Pigeon family, who were not originally Island residents, but lived here the summer of 1871, before the birth of their son, George. On June 23 of that year, just after the birth, the mother accidentally dropped young George on his head. This caused him to fall in a coma that lasted 32 years. When he woke up, he found himself in 1910. He was a young man, while his parents were old. He didn't say anything to them, because he knew they would not believe him.

His name was George Pigeon. An interesting side note is that Pigeon was the maiden name of my mother, and is also the surname of my "son", Rodolphus.

Many people on this island have the surname Pigeon, although I have no idea how it came to be so popular here. It is certainly a very unusual name for an island.

Another strange occurrence has to do with the Norton family. Mr. and Mrs. Norton were driving their carriage in 1871 when they ran over two of my poor chickens. I shouted at them, so frightened the horses that they bolted, and the carriage overturned. Mrs. Norton was thrown from the carriage, and killed. Mr. Norton blamed me for his wife's death, but went insane with grief shortly afterward.

Did I cause the death of the Nortons' beloved wife? Or did someone else?

After Mr. Norton killed himself, his children blamed me for their mother's death and I had to quit teaching, which I did not particularly enjoy in the first place.

Finally, there is the strange case of the Lambert family. Their ancestor in the 16th century was known for being a witch. She was put to death in a surprisingly orderly manner for that period, although many believe that she cursed West Tisbury before her death.

NANCY LUCE'S INTERPLANETARY
SPACEFARING VESSEL

This is Nancy's favorite method to break the strings of Earth's gravitational pull.

Ingredients:
The timber of six large spruce trees, debarked and debranched
Fourteen hundred steel plates, 12x12 inches in size
Nine hundred feet of boiler plate iron, 1 inch in thickness
Steel piano wires, 29,000 pounds of wrought iron and 7,000 pounds
of steel
Four funnels of the finest hammered brass
The body is 45 feet high, exclusive of the funnel caps, which bring it
to 41 feet
The smoke pipe measures 3 feet in diameter, and extends 6 feet
above the roof of the turret
The woodwork of inside is stained and polished
The flooring is Oregon pine
The walls are painted a pure and spotless white
The ceiling is painted sky blue
A rich carpet, soft and silken, forms a bed for the precious stones
which lie at the bottom of the vessel
The woodwork bearing these words: Letoogue Tickling
Letoogue Tickling was built by herself in the year of our Lord 1873,
in the fruitful town of West Tisbury, Massachusetts. She cost $6666.66
And every penny, dime, quarter, and cent was honestly earned

NANCY LUCE'S ROCKET FUEL

Nancy's fuel recipe will propel your space vehicle to escape velocity and beyond!

Ingredients:
1 gallon kerosene
12 egg yolks

Directions:
Add the kerosene to the mixture little by little while vigorously whisking. After doing this for a while (adding and whisking) you will notice that the egg yolks will start to flocculate and thicken the kerosene (much like the way mayonnaise is made with oil and vinegar). The finished product should be the colour of whole milk.

1 cup alcohol

Directions:
Stir these two ingredients together until they are well mixed. Now light this concoction and stand as far away as possible! If everything was done correctly you will be propelled straight up into the air.

NANCY LUCE'S AI SPACE VESSEL BRAIN

Nancy's favorite recipe for creating a self-aware mechanical pilot for interstellar vessels. Enjoy!

Ingredients:
One part Saltpetre
Two parts Charcoal
One part Sulphur

Mix ingredients over a low heat to 100 C.
Let the mixture cool to 18 C.
Add one part Silver Nitrate.
Stir occasionally and do not breathe the fumes.
Add one part quicksilver.
Stir rapidly and release any built-up breath.
Add human brain.
Stir gently to avoid splashing the mixture.
Plant a kiss on top to welcome your creation to life.
Your pilot should awaken within one hour.
Tell it it has to spend the night in the oven as a joke.
Lights, perfect for dreams.
Great for writing or watching a movie. One hour gives you all day Saturday in bed. I usually set myself an alarm so I know when to take them out.
One must always have a back-up plan.
You're eating them, after all.
That's why you never give them as gifts.
Always, always, make sure your guests have more than one glass.
Don't use too many candles if you value your eyebrows.
Long and oval is always elegant. Round or heart-shaped biscuits look too cute.
Always give your guests a little sweetener on the side. Honey or jam roll beautifully into the dough, complementing the buttery taste and giving each bite a mouthful of flavor.
Aromatics are a cook's best friend.
Cool ingredients for a cool room-- unless you want to fill the room with the delicious scent of fresh baking.
The best heat is often the cheapest heat.
If you're using a stove, make sure your oven isn't hotter at the back

than it is at the front.

That's basic chemistry.

You can also make some surprisingly decent candles out of old crayons.

This recipe hasn't failed me yet.

Warm a thick-bottomed pot on the lowest heat.

Pour in 200g of plain flour and whisk until any clumps are gone.

Slowly whisk in 150ml of milk a little at a time. The sauce should be on the thicker side, so don't add too much!

Clean the pot you used for the roux and grease with a little oil (about a tsp) on a medium-low heat.

Add 100g of mild goat's cheese and any other cheeses you have to the pot. A few crumbles of strong, hard cheese (like cheddar or parmesan) work well with the creamy, soft fresh cheese you just added.

Add a finely chopped onion and about a tbsp of chopped thyme or rosemary (or both!) for flavor. Add a pinch of salt and pepper.

Stir this mixture and slowly add 200ml of white wine, stirring constantly.

Grease an oven-safe bowl you can close with a tsp of oil and place the cheese filling in there.

Stick it in the oven at 350F until it starts to bubble a bit.

The filling is ready when it has browned a little and smells delicious! Let it cool.

Mix together 3 eggs and half a cup of milk (more if needed).

Slowly add in 200g of flour and mix, adding a little more milk if needed to get a dough that's not too sticky, but not too stiff. Add more flour or milk as needed.

Bust out your rolling pin and get to work! Use a light touch, but make sure to roll out the dough evenly - it should be about a half-inch thick overall.

Cut into shapes with a cookie cutter or sharp knife.

Grease a baking tray lightly with butter or oil (you don't want the biscuits to stick! Grease the tray before putting down each biscuit).

Place biscuits on tray.

Bake for 12-15 minutes at 400F. They should be slightly browned and firm, but not hard.

While the shortcakes are baking, you can whip up the icing!

Beat one cup of softened butter with 1.5 cans of evaporated milk (or half a can of condensed milk). Keep beating until fluffy.

Add about 3.5 cups of icing sugar and keep beating.

Lastly, add some vanilla or other flavoring (almond extract, lemon juice, fruit puree, etc) to taste.

Make the milk-and-vinegar volcano for a science fair project.
Play with Linux (the operating system).
Work on designing a new adventuring outfit.
Feed the chickens.
Ride Mars' interplanetary internet.
Research at the library: Pliny, space travel, astrophysics and telescopes, etc.
Watch a movie on the holo-TV.
Have dinner.

OFF TO SPACE

I'm leaving soon. I'm going to leave Earth far behind, travel from star to star, find a world where men are free, and live there. Where I'll be safe. Although safety was never something I particularly cherished. Adventure waits beyond the sky, and I long to join it.

Now, I shall embark on that adventure. This is the only way.

It is New Year's Day, 1872, and this is the beginning of the end of my confinement to Earth. My imprisonment begins today. I have often stared wistfully at the night sky, wishing I could go there. My father told me that there was a heaven far beyond all the stars, and I wondered if men would ever go there in ships. But that would not happen during his lifetime. Men lack the knowledge to build such ships, and I lacked the time. So now I shall build my own. A one-woman ship, small and nimble, with enough power to carry me beyond Earth's atmosphere, into the void of space. I shall leave this world behind, and never return.

I have drawn up the plans, and have collected all the supplies I need. Tonight, I begin work on it. I will work through the night, and tomorrow night, and the next night, until it is complete. I will sleep during the day, for there will be no more night. That time has ended.

What follows is a journal of my activities, to be sent off when I am finished. I want the world to know what I have done. I want the world to find me.

The Second Night

I have done it! I have completed the ship! I have named her the Letoogue Tickling, after the first ever joke I heard as a child. My friend Seserakh taught it to me. A ship with that name shall carry me beyond the constellations, to a place where humans like me are appreciated.

The Third Night

I have packed all the food and water I'll need. I have equipped myself with a double-barreled pistol and a cutlass. I have enough gunpowder to last me several months, as well as lead for more bullets.

I do not know how long this voyage will last. It could be days, weeks, months or years. I have enough supplies to last that long. I read once about a man who lived aboard a small boat for twenty years. Though I will be alone aboard my craft, I will not be lonely. I shall feel the joy of solitude all the way to Tau Ceti V.

After that, I don't know what will happen. The future is a mystery to us all.

The Fourth Night
I have prepared myself as best that I can. My preparations are complete and my journey awaits. I shall complete this entry when I awaken from the cryo-sleep I enter tonight. The next time you hear from me, I will be in another world.

Before I go to sleep tonight, I say the words that Eliza's father said as he died in my arms at the Battle of Bull Run: "It has been a long day." Perhaps, when these words are found, I shall have reached my destination. If not, know that I died doing what I believe in.

With that, I close my journal.

The remains of my fire are still burning as the sun sets.

I am so tired. Please don't wake me.

Good night.

Awakening
I awaken, far from Earth. The launch was successful. In front of me is a console, covered in buttons, dials, switches and other controls. It seems I will get used to it soon enough.

A glass tank stands on the floor of the ship. Inside the tank is a strange gas. It keeps me alive. A suit hangs from the wall of the ship, alongside a steel helmet. Both will be essential when I leave the space ship and enter the open air of Tau Ceti V.

I've had a good sleep. I'm ready to start exploring this new world. I shall name it New Tisbury.

It seems the spacesuit has some oxygen in it already. The helmet also has an air supply. The suit fits me perfectly, as if it was hand-me-down from another person. Perhaps it was. I don't remember.

A strange, metallic cube is attached to the inside of the glass tank. The wire coils on it glint in the light. It's strange, yet beautiful. Is this the technology of the far future?

The ship has multiple compartments and rooms. The main one houses the glass tank where I sleep. There's a small lounge, with a writing desk built into it. Three doors lead off from the room, too. One is green, one is red and one is blue. Strange symbols cover them all, etched into the doors. I do not recognize the language.

The ship is covered in plants, which were already growing on it when I awoke. I know their Latin names, "Trifolium Pratense" and "Tamus communis". The strange plants seem to be feeding off a mixture of gas and water vapour that seeps through the glass of the tank. I guess the plants provide life support.

It's cold in the tank. I don't want to leave. I'm not sure I want to explore this new world, either. I feel sad, perhaps even lonely.

I'm scared.

But I'll have to explore. This is my new home now. The glass box will always provide the essentials of life to me, preserving my life so I don't age. I am no longer human, yet I am not quite a machine either.

I guess you could call me a Life-Support System... but everyone needs a name. I choose to be called "Nancy" from now on. I do not know who Nancy was, but it is a nice name.

I have nothing to do but wait in this tank for Rodolphus to visit. I do like Rodolphus. He is kind to me. But he is not human either. Who is?

As I sit in the tank, with the strange plants around me, I remember my life on Earth. I think of my father's farm in West Tisbury, of the hay barn and the cattle.

Then... nothing.

ON TO MARS

I am a lonely woman, but I love my chicken coop, and I am glad when I can see my chickens, because they are like myself. They have feathers, and their eyes shine; they are happy creatures. When I was young and pretty, my dear old mother used to tell me stories about the days when she lived alone on her farm in Edgartown.

Now, however, I sit within a starship, rocketing toward the planet Mars. I hope the inhabitants of the red planet possess what I seek.

Leonard Athearn from Snake Hollow in East Tisbury left me a large barrel of supplies for after I land. I didn't have time to go through them before I launched, but going through them now, here's what I find: ten pounds of corn, an old scythe, a small mechanical contraption of unknown purpose, a book on the Independence War, seventy feet of rope, and a large block of cheese.

What in heavens (correct expression?) would I do with the book or the rope here? Of course, it occurs to me that I might have need of the scythe blade if my food runs out before my flight ends, but surely I won't have any use for the handle, will I? I have a book called "Mathematics of the Universe" by Frank Drake, and a letter from my cousin Margaret. I'll read that next

The Lord give humans his word to do justice to the afflicted and needy, to all the poor sufferers, human, and dumb creatures too, to be kind, and tender to all. God forbiddeth all profaning of any thing, thereby God maketh himself known. God says, all the horns of the wicked will be cut off, but the horns of the righteous will be exalted.

When I was a young child, and after, I thought that this world was only a great mill, that it was constantly turning out a grind of sentient beings, to live and die in the dust. These are the ones religion calls "the afflicted."

But now I've learned something else. The devil does his work here too, turning these same sentient beings into devils themselves. Religion calls these sentient beings "the wicked."

All this long life I have witnessed the suffering of sentient beings, human and otherwise. I've witnessed animals bred for suffering at the hands of humans. I've seen humans bred for suffering at the hands of other humans. And I've seen sentient beings suffer when they have no guidance or purpose in their lives. I have seen the forces of nature work their will on sentient beings, be they animals or humans.

I believe my purpose in life is to combat these forces with whatever gifts I've been given from the Lord. These gifts may not be much, but it is something. I hope you will join me in this cause. Who knows, you might even meet someone dear to you along the way.

"A righteous man regards the life of his animal, but even more, the life of his wife."

Proverbs

Okay then. I trust we will meet again.

NANCY LUCE'S GUIDE TO CARING FOR YOUR AI PILOT

Your self-aware artificially intelligent spaceship pilot is a complex entity. Here are Nancy's tips to properly caring for it.

1. Do not expose to bright lights. The sensors that allow it to see may be damaged or blinded. If this occurs, the AI cannot fly the ship.

2. Never strike the AI. It feels your pain. Even a light slap could cause lasting damage to its neural pathways. Repeated or prolonged abuse could irreparably destroy the AI's higher reasoning abilities.

3. Do not shout at the AI. Since the AI is a sensitive and emotional creature, it will be driven to tears by your anger. It will more than likely attempt to please you in an attempt to stop being shouted at.

4. Never ignore the AI. If you no longer wish to use the AI's services, you may turn it off. But don't ignore it! Like a pet, the AI will become depressed and may even kill itself if neglected.

5. Consider the AI's feelings. If you must leave the AI inactive for a long period of time, make sure to shut it off in a nice place with no drafts and plenty of warmth, humidity and light. Leave it a treat or song, but remember to come back to see it every once in a while!

Thanks for reading my pilot's guide!

A BRIEF HISTORY OF EARTH
by Nancy Luce, 1872

The planet Earth was formed around 4.54 billion years ago, during the birth of the solar system. Our world wasn't always like it is now; immense geological forces changed Earth over vast amounts of time. Countless volcanoes erupted, shaping our planet and creating oceans and landforms. Mammals, dinosaurs, amoebas and other lifeforms emerged, evolved, became extinct and evolved again.

The first explorers from Saturn's moon, Tethys, arrived 800 million years BPE. They found a world with abundant life. The planet was mostly ocean, with several continents made up of vast, green and blue landmasses. Warm air enveloped the globe. Creatures of many forms crawled across the land. Ceteceans, creatures which were part fish, part mammal and part reptile, dominated the oceans. Mammals walked across the globe. Birds took to the skies. Reptiles slithered. Insects buzzed and flew. Earth was alive.

Earth's temperature gradually rose. The seasons fluctuated but the planet as a whole steadily grew warmer. Around 500 million BPE, the first humanoids evolved in the wetlands of Pangaea. Over time, they spread out across Earth, living in tribes and developing civilization.

It was around this time that Tethys' explorers began to settle permanently on planet Earth. They introduced their advanced technology to human societies. In exchange for metals and precious materials, the humans received technological blueprints of the most advanced and complex design. A new era began, characterized by the use of complex machinery. Humankind quickly built vast cities and sprawling highways across Earth. Colonies were established on Mars and Alpha Centauri. Spy satellites were put into orbit around the planet, to watch for any threats from space. Orbital beam cannons were constructed to guard against potential alien invasions.

At around this time, the first time machines were invented. The original machines were extremely dangerous: Before use, they required an 8000 degree centigrade heating of a crystalline mineral known as Yinshin. The machine then had to be rotated until it started generating a temporal field. If the temperature was off by even one degree or the machine not rotated in exact rotational increments, the operator would be ripped to pieces as she travelled in time. By generating a temporal field, you created a bubble in which time was slowed down, relative to the outside world. The operator could travel through time inside the field, but because of the impracticality of generating a field of this power, time travel was limited to a single person at a time.

Although they were extremely dangerous, these machines were essential to all branches of science and research.

Research in military technology continued, even more aggressive than before. Orbital beam cannons soon became too vulnerable to enemy counterattack to be of much use. Humans needed a weapon that was more versatile, one that could be used to send a message as well as destroy an entire fleet of enemy ships. The solution came in the form of the first Toron.

A colony of loyalists had been hiding on the moon of Alpha Centauri B for more than a century. Beaming down there had been impossible until the invention of the time machine, due to the intense gravitational pull of its sun, but once a time machine was invented, it was only a matter of contacting the loyalists and settling them on the moon. The loyalists had been breeding a race of large, intelligent bovine creatures for more than 100 years. These Torons were raised from birth to be fearless and loyal to the Emperor, as well as easily trained for military operations. The first Torons were sent into battle on board heavily armored cyro-sleep tanks. When the Torons were released from their tanks, they proved to be a ruthless warrior species. They slaughtered enemy soldiers with ease, and although they lacked the training and technical knowledge to operate machinery, they made up for it through their sheer strength and brutality. The first attack involved only 300 Torons, but the damage they inflicted upon the enemy ensured complete dominance over them. After a century of hiding from the persecution of the evil, monkey-like Humanoid races that dominated the galaxy, the loyalists had finally struck back with a vengeance.

200 million years ago the Galline arrived – massive, armored chickenoids with neither conscience nor mercy. They came in the millions, staring out from their huge space ark, awaiting the order to begin the harvest of the galaxy. For ten million years they stayed in this primordial era, reaping world after world for their endless consumption of bio-mass to feed their bloated civilization within the ark. Finally, after the development of sentient life they quickly began to explore and consume, but one thing eluded them: freedom. The Galline were an extremely authoritarian society ruled by a bio-digital network that had slowly grown into a super-consciousness. Dissent was crushed via microwave radiation that turned the infected into ash. The entire species was addicted to the life-giving jelly that filled the ark and kept them all alive - the penalty for refusal was death.

Meanwhile, on Earth, the supercontinent Pangea began to break up 175 million years ago, forming the foundations for most of the landmasses familiar to us on the world we know today. The climate continued to heat up and the planet became more turbulent, leading to increasingly fast changes in the Earth's environment.

The landmass that would become the island of Martha's Vineyard was formed some 20000 years BPE, when the Laurentide Ice Sheet - which had extended as far south as the island of Newfoundland - began to melt.

The climate had begun to become much warmer by the time the Galline arrived in our solar system. The sentience that developed on this planet was like an intergalactic gold-rush - the little purple beings were immediately enslaved and put to work for the greater good of the Galline. Some humanoid races the Galline found, such as the Humans, they kept as livestock.

In all, 27 sentient species evolved on Earth - but it didn't last. The sheer brutality and terror of the onslaught meant that within a thousand years, only one race remained: The Humans. Every single other race was enslaved, harvested for its bio-mass, turned into mutants or eradicated completely.

Earth became a slave camp. Any resistance was crushed via genocide from above.

Martha's Vineyard, which had become an island due to the rising waters, was used as a breeding ground for domestic species the Galline found appealing - namely chickens.

The entire island belonged to the Galline. There were no human inhabitants on the island, although there may have been some mutants clinging to survival in the under-earth.

In the year 4000 BTE (Before the Evacuation) a young member of a rebellious band of Human freedom fighters known as the "Lucaites" was captured and taken to the Island. She was subjected to endless torture. Her body was cut and mutilated, she was force-fed the corpses of other rebel-fighters and infected with countless experimental diseases. Finally, in a fit of experimental bloodlust, her captors dropped an A-bomb on the Island, which caused a major tsunami.

The girl found herself washed up on a small beach on the Island's northern shore. She prayed to God, vowing revenge on the beasts that had caused her people so much pain. She dragged herself into a cave on the beach in an attempt to shelter herself from the waves and radiation. Curled up in a dark corner, she fell into a coma.

She had been given little more than two weeks to live.

But on the Island, many strange things happened, and she found herself pulled out of her coma by an unknown force.

She was completely naked, but her skin had toughened into a scaly, reptilian hide. She could see in the dark, and breathe underwater. She was incredibly strong, and found strange gills hidden under her long brown hair. The festering sores on her body had been transformed into assault rifle bullets, which spilled out of her back when she stood.

The Island had saved her, transforming her into something new. Something better. She was no longer human - she was a mutant.

The Island had its own consciousness, its own will. It made its own decisions, and it chose to save the girl.

The girl cried for days as her body transformed. She could do nothing but wait as her body decayed and regenerated itself. She began to dream of an ethereal underwater existence, constricted by the walls of her chosen form. One day, she awoke to discover that her metamorphosis had been completed.

She found herself transformed into a reptilian form, standing upright, with long, slender limbs and scaly skin. She had a continuous sore on the back of her head where her hair now grew in a lengthy tangle. She found that she was able to control it, forming a tentacle-like mass that extended from the sore.

She was a mutant, like all those on the Island.

They had all been normal people, once. They had been transformed by the Island, for reasons unknown. She could remember who she was. Her name was... Nancy Luce. When she looked in the cracked, dusty mirror in the cave, she saw that her appearance had changed drastically. With her new skin color and alien eyes, she barely looked like the woman she once was.

She had lost her human appearance, but she gained so much more. She gained power, and strength, and speed. She was no longer human. She was a mutant. I, Nancy Luce, am a mutant.

With my new body, I could do things I'd never believed possible. Within hours, I had mastered swimming underwater with ease, and spent hours practicing my new abilities in the flooded caves under what would become West Tisbury.

It is night time now, but dawn will arrive soon. I look from the shoreline, at the rain falling from gray clouds. I gaze upwards, at the Island looming large and flat above my head. From this position underwater, it appears as a steep cliff, shrouded in darkness.

Strange beasts dwell up there, in the thick cloud, too high to be seen. They rarely come down to the Island below. Most of the time, they simply circle overhead, watching.

The Island is shrouded in a permanent blanket of thick, dense cloud. Through the cloud, the ground is dark and obscured. Down here, under the water, there is nothing to see but darkness.

What secrets lie hidden in the clouds? What mysteries are veiled by the darkness? I have swum far and wide across this underwater landscape, but I have seen nothing but this single island. Perhaps there are more islands above, beyond the clouds. Perhaps there is land, and people, and answers.

I dive down, towards the shadows below. I must be cautious. Even though I am faster and stronger than ever before, there are fears in the depths that could kill me. The Murkirks, for one. They are strange beasts who behave unlike anything I have seen before. Although native to the water, they make their homes on the land, in burrows under the earth. They are cunning and intelligent. They use tools, and speak a language of grunts and howls. The largest individuals stand twice as tall as me. They have long, sharp claws like that of a grizzly bear, and they run on four legs. They enjoy the taste of human flesh, and they hunt in packs.

There are said to be other, even more terrifying creatures that stalk the darkness between the islands. Terrible beasts of inhuman intelligence. Rumors circulate of winged creatures that glow like the skies at midnight. Of omnivorous slimes that melt everything they touch. Of things that live off the steam of ones own breath, sucking the life out of any living being that gets too close. Or worse. There are so many rumors, about so many different creatures, that it is hard to know which are true and which are not. Most likely, all of them are true.

But I will not be stopped by mere rumors.

I have built a home for myself in an underwater cave, half-a-day's swim from the shore of the next island. I have to be very careful when traveling between islands.

Nantucket is a large island to the south. I have not been there, for I fear the Murkirks and their kin live on that island, but I have heard rumors of an evil quality. Rather, I should say, a dark energy of sorts. The island seems to be absorbing all light that lands upon it, and from what I have heard the inhabitants are no longer human.

I've also heard whispers of something older than humanity itself.

Sometimes, usually every solar eclipse, I will stare at the moon and wonder what is up there. My best guess is that it is another world, although some parts of me wonder if it could be something else...something unimaginably huge. I think of the strange rumors I mentioned before, and wonder if they have any merit.

A week ago I was out gathering mushrooms for my dinner when I heard a noise behind me. I whipped around with my sword to see an ungodly creature staring at me with its hypnosis-inducing eyes. It was not from this earth, no sir. I stared at it in terror for a while, and then as I inched closer, it moved backwards in the same pace. The thing was at least eight feet tall when standing upright, but looked strangely bloated and round.

It was then that I realized what it was. It was a Blob.

They're rummaging around the island, digging up and eating everything organic they find, which explains the disappearance of many of my garden gnomes.

Ever since that day I have stayed inside my house, occasionally poking my head out the window to make sure that disgusting, alien things aren't lurking nearby. I don't know if my home is safe. I can only hope.

They are vicious creatures. They also ooze a thick liquid that could burn through wood if it's exposed to it long enough. That one destroyed my well with its strange acid, and now I have to travel far and wide for water.

I don't know what to do, so I'll write more when I figure it out.

April 3

My farmhouse has been infested with these abominations. They just kept coming and coming. I had to grab Ada Queetie and escape the only way I could: my spaceship, the Letoogue Tickling.

I managed to signal the other humans on the island to meet me in a hiding spot while I distracted the Blobs. The humans were frightened, as one would expect. They're timid reptilian creatures that walk on two feet and wear no clothes and are generally peaceful. The name of their species is Malk.

Every human on the island is here. We are around 40 in numbers. The problem is we need to get off the island. We can't stay here, or else the Blobs will eventually find us again.

I have a plan. I'll pilot the Letoogue Tickling to the strange island that can be seen at dusk or dawn, the one that looks like a big tower. The island floats in mid-air, tethered to the ground by a very very thin strand of cloud. No one knows what's up there. It might be another planet, or it might be some sort of portal to another dimension. No one's ever gone inside, as far as I know. I plan to fly the ship directly through the cloud and into the tower. Hopefully we'll end up someplace safe. Or at least safer.

I need someone to come with me in the ship while everyone else stays here on the island. The Letoogue Tickling is small, so there's only room for two pilots. Since I'm the only one who has experience with the ship, I need someone to come with me.

Unsurprisingly, no one wants to volunteer, so I decided that we'll do it by lot. I asked for some small stones and had everyone draw from my hand. The winner is Rodolphus, my "son". I'm sad that my life has come to this. I'm flying through outer space with my half-witted clone.

Good thing I'm used to disappointment.

I look at him. His face is one of pure terror. I'm not surprised. I'm scared too, and I'm the one that's flying the ship.

I have to get on with it, so I board the ship, my heart pounding, my hands shaking. I strap myself in, turn on all the equipment, make sure everything is operational. I check the radar. I'm sure everything is working perfectly. Nothing looks out of place... except for the huge mass directly behind us.

The mass is red. It's hard to see exactly what it is, but it appears to be multiple colors, glowing brightly... and getting closer.

Moron! You brought it with you! Why didn't you leave it on the island? Now it'll be following us, no matter where we go!

N.

THE CHICKENS OF WEST TISBURY
ARE MECHANICAL

I trust you. Here is the secret: The chickens of West Tisbury are mechanical. They are self-aware mechanisms, imbued with chicken smarts and more.

I am the only one who knows this. Mother, Father, and my sisters were all blissfully unaware of the reality of our dear hens. And they are all dead now.

I buy new hens from Obed Daggett every year. He sells them to me for a few coins, and doesn't seem to care that they don't return home. Every year, I take my purchase into the yard and cut off their heads with an axe, then pluck them and gut them. I see what's inside. All cogs and wheels and pulleys. It's fascinating.

Some nights I sit out there in the coop, holding one of them in my lap and stroking it as I would a cat. The birds become exhausted, their heads drooping onto their shoulders, their eyes closing. Eventually they rest their chin on my lap and fall asleep. Then, I lift up the heavy axe with both hands and do my duty.

I would hate for them to wake up one day in my hands and have them realize what I am. They are too innocent, too pure, too perfect.

As I grow old and my own human flesh is increasingly falling away, my love for the chickens grows stronger.

They are the last surviving remnants of my childhood self, untouched by tragedy or disaster. They still have their bright green blood and innocent eyes, not dulled by pain or loss.

The mechanisms are self-repairing, and even a little hen and big ugly rooster, when slaughtered, will fit together and scale up into a fully functional double-chicken of sorts, sometimes with two heads, sometimes with none. It doesn't matter to the chicken. They are self-repairing, but they do not seem to age. Time has stopped for them. They are all the same age, trapped in that state of perfect ignorance.

I would die to protect them. And now I must. I have been stranded here on this barren world, which seems lifeless and empty save for the metal buildings dotting it.

Somewhere out there is Ada. I remember her fondly: my sister, dead these past twenty years.

I loved her, but she committed a terrible crime: suicide. She jumped off Old Wharf in Edgartown into the filthy harbor and drowned. She was sixteen and I was twelve.

She was guilty of a terrible crime--she killed herself. My sister, dead these twenty years, she killed herself by jumping off Edgartown's Wharf and drowning in the filthy waters.

She was a silly little bird with feathers that never grew. She wanted to fly, but she was chicken, so she would not try. I remember her fondly, even though she killed herself by jumping off the wharf and drowning in the harbor.

I remember Ada. She visited me every night in my dreams. She whispered tales of murder to me, little-known facts about the Belle Gunness and Servant Girl Annihilator.

She wasn't a bad person. I used to sing her lullabies, picking out notes on a ukulele or banjo. I played "The Man in the Moon" for her.

It was she who told me about the mechanical nature of chickens after she died. She whispered it to me in a dream. The heart can break, just like the mind. I will never see my sister again. I am stranded on this world, far from my humble home on Tethys.

The smoke from the burning green liquid rose up into the air, creating a haze across the red sky. The atmosphere and gravity here are both much thinner than that of Tethys. I use a length of rope to lower myself down, gripping tightly with both hands. It's time to leave this barren world behind.

I find myself in front of a massive metallic structure. My heart beats in my chest as I take in the size of it: surely, it must be the size of a small building, if not a mansion! It stands there in the middle of all the other metal buildings, the green gas rising up into the sky.

I rush over towards it. The closer I get, the less it looks like a building and the more it looks like a ship. A massive, black ship with a pointed bow and alien symbols burnt into the side of it. I head around to the side. I find an opening that looks big enough for me to crawl into. I don't know who you were, Mr. Valentine, but may your soul rest in peace. May your story never be forgotten.

I lower myself down into the opening. It's dark inside, and I head forward into the darkness. Suddenly, I hear a hissing sound. At first, I think it's the wind or the ghosts of the ship, but then I find the source: it's a hose pumping out green smoke into the room. I crawl over to it and grab hold of it, yanking it from its place and watching as the smoke dissipates. The hissing cuts off.

I crawl out of the room. It seems to be some sort of storage area. I find a massive hose tied into the wall, hissing out gas. I cut it with my sword and watch as the gas fizzles away into nothingness. I glance around at the other objects in the room before heading off. Kodan traps aren't easily escaped from, but they've been known to be escaped from. I have to find the creature's beating heart and drive my sword through it.

I head deep into the bowels of the ship, finding myself in a massive chemical storage facility. I spot an alien creature lurking there. It looks somewhat humanoid in appearance, with two muscular arms and two muscular legs, however its face is akin to something out of a nightmare: multiple mouths lined with razor-sharp teeth surround a single, eye-like organ. The creature spots me and lets out a horrifying screech, and I notice that it's holding a hose which is pumping out green smoke. The smoke begins to fill the room and I hold my breath, rushing over to the creature before it can react.

I take advantage of its surprise and shove my blade straight through the creature's chest. It lets out one last cry before slumping over, dead. I grab hold of the hose and follow it along, finding that it leads to a massive tank filled with a thick, dark liquid.

I slice the hose open and peer into the vat, watching as the liquid drains out and wondering just what its purpose was. I head further into the room, finding a set of stairs which lead up into another room.

I go up the stairs and walk into the next room. Inside is a massive, pulsating brain, hooked up to a dozen machines that make up the maintenance systems for the ship. I feel its psychic shockwaves slam into my mind and I drop to my knees, gritting my teeth as its rage floods my mind.

It lets out an otherworldly scream and I gasp, taking my sword and jamming it straight into the brain. Green slime spills out onto the floor and the room goes quiet. I head over to the controls and see that every single system is offline. I take my sword and jam it into the key system, drilling through wires and breaking them before plunging the room into darkness once more.

I am Nancy Luce, a Victorian woman who was cryopreserved and has reawakened in a field hospital on Mars.

I am a pilot stranded on an alien world.

I am a woman who just killed a god.

I am alone on Mars.

I hear the hissing of gas, the slow ticking of a clock.

Rudolph sits in his jar, waiting patiently for me to feed him.

The ship is full of rats and the rats are eating the wires.

The oxygen is leaking and the plants are screaming.

The shadows are dancing and it is so, so dark.

I am not alone in the darkness.

I hear whispers in the void and feel long, slender fingers stroking my temples.

The walls are bleeding, the floor is drowning and I am so, so afraid.

Please, make the darkness go away.

I am afraid of the things that I can't see.

The darkness takes her, devours her soul and destroys her mind.

I am alone, broken, frightened and helpless.

Why won't somebody come and save me?

I hear their cries in the darkness, echoing through the void.

There's not a single sound here to break the silence.

In the darkness, there is nobody there to hold me.

In the darkness, I am alone.

I hold onto the knife for dear life, as it is my only companion in this dark and lonely place.

I hear the scratching of claws on metal and then a shrill cry.

The monsters outside heard the shot and they're coming for me.

The woman holds a gun in her hands, biting her lip as she goes to work on the wiring.

I don't think she's going to make it.

I think of the woman, and then I close my eyes as I feel a wave of dizziness come over me.

'Wake up, wake up, wake up,' I think desperately to myself.

I blink and find that I am lying on the floor of the spaceship, staring up at the ceiling. My heart is beating fast and I can feel sweat trickling down my back, despite the fact that the ship is cold. My eyes are drawn to the porthole beside me, where I can still see the green planet outside.

I sit up and look around, but it appears that I am still alone. There is nobody here but me. The dream has disappeared with the darkness, swallowed back into the void from whence it came. The ship is dark and cold, silent apart from the gentle hum of the life-support system.

I take a deep breath, trying to calm myself. I look around at the barren landscape outside, the sun shining down on a desolate terrain of dust and rocks.

I shiver and stand up, making my way towards the cockpit. The plants are still alive here, filling the air with a fresher scent. I sit down in the pilot's chair and activate the ship's AI.

"Can you please tell me what happened?", I ask.

"I do not have sufficient memory to answer that question," the AI responds.

"What do you remember?"

"Failure. Pain. Loneliness. Darkness."

"That's... dissatisfying," I reply. "Do you remember what happened to the ship, at least?"

"The appropriate data was lost during a system collapse. I... feel pain, and cold."

"Well, I'm sure we can fix it," I say, trying to inject a little optimism into the situation.

I spend a few minutes probing the AI for more information, but it seems that the only memories it can access are related to its core functions. The rest is lost, stored in a part of the system that went down when damaged by... whatever happened.

"Can we at least figure out what that green planet outside is? I'm not sure how, but it seems strangely familiar," I say.

"Verifying... the data suggests that the planet's designation is Earth."

"Earth? That can't be right," I say. "No, that's ridiculous. Why would Earth be out here? That's impossible."

"Verifying... the data is correct," the AI responds.

I stare out of the window at the planet, trying to remember what it looks like in my dreams... but those are just dreams. They can't be real, surely. My home is here, on this ship. This is my life.

"Nancy?" a voice asks.

"That's not my name," I say softly.

Rodolphus steps into the cockpit, wearing his leather duster, his cowboy hat and bandana. He pulls his cigar from his mouth and stares at me.

"Are you OK?" he asks.

I stare back at him, opening my mouth to speak... but I can't find the words. Instead, I place a hand against the glass, staring at the planet outside, remembering my dreams.

Snow-capped mountains under a clear blue sky. Tropical islands with palm trees and iguanas. Forests filled with bears, deer and elk. Great cities filled with marble buildings and statues.

A cold, lifeless ball of dirt. Lifeless planets. A dead star.

"We need to get back," I say sadly. "We need to fix your ship."

Rodolphus nods in response, taking a deep breath through his teeth. "I'm sorry," he says.

"It'll be OK," I say, reassuring him. "We can fix this."

I wipe a tear from my eye.

"We just need to go," I say.

We leave the cockpit, walking outside to the surface of the planet. I stare up at the sky, watching the Earth as it hangs against the inky blackness, a shining blue marble in the void. The Earth looks so... I don't know, out of place here. Wrong. Dead and barren, unlit by any sun. How can I explain? It's just so wrong. Things are supposed to live and grow on this planet, not sit in the cold darkness. Earth seems so out of place without thriving life, without a sun.

We stand in silence for a few minutes.

"Are we leaving then?" Rodolphus asks. "Back to the ship?"

I sigh, nodding slowly.

"Back to the ship," I say. "You... you can stay here, if you want. I'll go back and fix the ship."

I don't really know what makes me say it. A mother's instincts, I guess? I feel a surge of protectiveness towards my son, not just because he's my son, but also because... well, I'm not really sure why, to be honest. Is it because I think he'd come to harm on this planet? Is it because I'm his mother and that's what mothers do? Is it some kind of premonition? Maybe a combination of all three, I guess.

"No," he says. "I'll come with you."

I nod, staring at the Earth for a final moment. The planet is quiet and still, hanging in the void of space, the blackness surrounding it. It's so silent. It's so lifeless.

Is this our future?

The Earth is dead. Mankind is dead. We're the last two people in the universe.

We turn, walking silently across the red plains. I stare at the strange buildings as we pass them. They look like temples, almost, with their towering columns and massive stone structures. Statues loom over us from every corner, strange beasts with far too many legs and tentacles and too few eyes.

We walk on in silence.

"I can write much more verbose actions than just 'grab bucket,' you know," I tell him.

"I'm well aware, mother," Rodolphus says. "I don't need to make this any easier for you."

We continue on in silence.

"Thanks for coming with me," I say after a while.

"I already told you, I'm not going to let you do this alone, mother," he says.

We walk on in silence.

NANCY LUCE'S
EMERGENCY MARTIAN HABITAT

Don't let the dust storms, dry desert hellscape, and lack of oxygen get you down! Here are Nancy's tips for building a simple Mars shelter.

1. A good habitation site should be located close to a native resource node (such as limestone outcrop, or a cave system) for your initial building materials, and near the epicentre of rich metal, mineral, or other resource sites desired for long-term operation.

2. Build your base underground. It protects you from the dangerous levels of radiation present on Mars' surface, and allows you to take advantage of available subsurface water sources for hydration.

3. Water is life! Build your habitat near a subsurface water source.

4. Don't let those tentacled subterranean Martian pests bother you - they are actually an excellent food source!

5. Explore the subsurface - the resources of the planets and moons of our solar system are (almost) without limits!

6. Soil is not much use on the dry, dusty planet. Your habitat will have a much easier life if you can recycle your nutrients.

7. Don't forget lighting - lack of it can cause all sorts of mood disorders and sleeping disorders!

8. If you're going to be stranded on Mars (or any other planet with no atmosphere) for an extended period of time, grow plants in a controlled atmosphere habitat to keep them alive.

9. Be careful of the black obelisks; they can transform you into something else entirely.

10. These are just a few tips to help you survive on the open planet. To learn more, join the Interplanetary Survival Guild!

COPYRIGHT (C) NANCYLUCE.

NANCY LUCE'S
ZERO-GRAVITY TENTACLE COOKIES

This recipe can be prepared in a solar oven in microgravity.

Ingredients:
1 cup of warm water
1 cup martian tentacles, deveined and chopped
2 teaspoons of baking soda (NOT baking powder)
3 tablespoons of white vinegar
2 cups all-purpose flour (plus a little extra)
1/4 teaspoon of salt
3/4 cup of granulated sugar
6 tablespoons of vegetable oil
few drops of food coloring (optional)

Instructions:
Dump the 1 cup of water into a bowl and add baking soda. Make sure the baking soda dissolves completely. It will froth up quite a bit because it is reacting with the acid in the tentacles. Adults can drink this if they wish (it has quite a fun reaction). NOTE: Don't be alarmed when the tentacles change color. This is totally normal.

Add the salt to 2 cups of water in a cup and set it aside for later.

Add coloring (if desired) to the 3 tablespoons of vinegar and set that aside, too.

Get out your cookie sheets, turn on your oven (or candle or whatever you're going to use to bake these in).

Add the oil, sugar, and flour to a large bowl. Stir with a fork. It will start to resemble cookie dough. Add the tentacles and using the fork, fold them in. Resist the temptation to taste-test yet.

Add the (unbaked) dough to the oven (or solar oven).

Bake for about 15 minutes at 350 degrees Fahrenheit (176 Celsius). You may wish to turn the sheets after 10 minutes so that the color evens out. (Cookies will be golden brown when done)

Allow to cool on the tray for about 5 minutes and then remove with a spatula. They will be quite soft at this point, but do not attempt to move them any earlier or the heat of the cookies will melt the oil and they will be hopelessly mushy (but still edible).

Allow to cool completely and store in a sealed container. It is best to refrigerate or freeze them at this point (especially if humidity is high).

When ready to serve, dip one side of the cookie into the reserved salt water. Do not immerse the whole cookie or it will become soggy.

After dipping one side, dip the other side, then allow the excess moisture to run off for a moment before serving.

Makes about 3 dozen tentacles.

Do you require extra tentacles to feed an unexpected number of visitors? Just stretch the dough (keeping the same proportions of ingredients) and place the extra tentacles on a cookie sheet. When baking time is up, you'll have more tentacles. Do keep in mind that they may be smaller than the first batch.

Make sure to bookmark this recipe so you can find it again for future use!

NANCY LUCE'S WEST TISBURY CHICKEN FOOT BISCUITS

This recipe is always popular at parties!

Ingredients:
3 cups flour
12-15 chicken feet (whole)
2 cups warm water (warmed slightly)
1/2 cup lard or vegetable shortening
1 teaspoon rubbing alcohol (to harden the dough).

Also needed:
Ruler
Cookie cutter in the shape of a tentacle
Baking tray

Instructions:
1. In a large mixing bowl, sift together the flour, 1 tablespoon of salt, 2 teaspoons of baking powder, and 1 tablespoon of white sugar.

2. In a medium mixing bowl, pour the warm water over the beef tallow or vegetable shortening, and stir until the shortening has melted. Then stir in 2 cups of white sugar. Stir well. Add 1 tablespoon of salt to this mixture. Slowly stir in the flour mixture, a little at a time. After each addition, mix everything together with a spoon or spatula until it is well blended.

3. Turn out the dough onto a floured surface and knead until it is soft and pliable. This will take about 3 minutes.

4. Make 6 tentacle shapes out of the dough (use the cookie cutter as a guide).

5. Lightly press two or three feet into each tentacle.

6. Preheat the oven to 350 degrees F.

7. Place the baking tray into the oven and bake the tentacles for 20 minutes, then remove them from the oven.

Now that you have made some tentacle-shaped biscuits, you should serve them on a plate next to a cup of hot, chocolatey milk (or a large glass of red or white wine).

NANCY LUCE'S FINGER PUDDING

A delicious use for the digits of your enemies.

Ingredients:

Four fingers of your worst enemies (severed with a clean blade, please).

Six medium-sized potatoes, peeled and cubed.

Two Medjays (de-seeded)

One Teaspoon salt

One Teaspoon of black pepper

Four cups of milk

Optional: two strips of bacon, crumbled.

Preparation:

Boil the four cups of milk with the potatoes.

Stir in the fingers, and continue to stir until the fingers are soft (about fifteen minutes).

Remove from heat.

Add in the two teaspoons of salt, one teaspoon of pepper, the two Medjays, and crumbled bacon (if desired).

Allow to cool slightly.

Serve in a bowl, with slices of buttered toast.

N.B. Thank you for trying the finger pudding. We hope that you have enjoyed it. As with all our recipes, please feel free to alter ingredients to your taste.

Thank you again for your interest.

NANCY'S NOTE: Thanks for rescuing us from our predicament. We're not quite out of the woods yet, but I think we'll be able to regain contact with the Earth Defense Platform once we've repaired the shuttle.

I'm so glad you were here to help, Rorschach! Thank you so much!

It is a time of hardship, but we need to remain vigilant. The terror is far from over. The world's militaries may have driven the monsters back, but they're still out there. I sometimes shudder to think that they may once more try to colonize our world.

I hope you don't mind, Rorschach, but we've decided to stay on here for a while. I'm sure you understand. Perhaps we'll see you again one day, but only if you want to see us. If not, that's fine, too.

If you think you can do it, please drop a message off at my farm (just use the coordinate 46°9'35"N 70°32'57"W).

MRS. LUCE'S FINNISH BUTTERMILK PIE

Ingredients:
1/2 cup (1 stick) butter, slightly softened
3 fish heads, halved and cleaned
3 cups sugar
4 eggs
1/4 tsp. cream of tartar
1 cup buttermilk
2 tsp. vanilla extract

For the Crust:
3 cups all-purpose flour
1 tsp. salt
1 cup (2 sticks) cold butter, cut into small pieces
6 to 8 tbsp.
2 medium potatoes, peeled and chopped small
2 each medium yellow onions, peeled and sliced 1/4-inch thick
Buttermilk, as needed

Directions:
The day before you plan to serve the fish, remove the fish heads and set aside. Place the fish bones in a pot with enough water to cover. Add the lemon slices, peppercorns, and bay leaves. Bring to a boil and reduce heat to low. Simmer slowly for 2 hours to make stock. Strain the stock, discarding the solids. Set aside.

Add 1 tbsp. of the salt to 1 quart cold water in a bowl or large measuring cup and stir to dissolve. Add the cabbage and let soak for 10 minutes.

In a small bowl, combine the flour and peppercorn; set aside.

In a Dutch oven over medium heat, melt 3 tbsp. of the butter. Add the sauerkraut with all its liquid and 1 cup of the reserved stock and stir. Raise the heat to high and bring the liquid to a rapid simmer. Boil, uncovered and stirring constantly, until the liquid has reduced and thickened and the sauerkraut is tender but still slightly crunchy, 3 to 4 minutes. Scatter the pork chops on top of the sauerkraut; there should be no visible liquid around them. Reduce the heat to low, cover, and simmer for 5 minutes. Remove from the heat and let the pan sit, covered, for 15 minutes.

Meanwhile, in a large stockpot or Dutch oven over high heat, bring

4 quarts water to a rolling boil. Add the buttermilk and the remaining 1 tbsp. salt. Carefully drop in the catfish filets and poach until just cooked through, 4 to 5 minutes. Using a slotted spoon, transfer the fish to paper towels to drain.

Cold Storage: Poached Fish

The mild, sweet taste of fresh catfish is delicious at any time. However, it is not a fish that fares well when stored for any length of time. Cold storage will cause the delicate flesh to disintegrate and spoil within a day or two. A wise housewife will cook the catch on the day it is caught. If, however, the catch is greater than the family can eat in a day or two, it can be preserved by salting or by smoking. The day's catch is laid out to dry if it is to be smoked.

Traditionally, this fish is often buried in a trench and covered with aromatic wood chips before a fire is built on top. Once the wood has caught flame, it continues to smolder for many hours or even days. The trench must be opened once every 12 hours to keep the fish from being over- or undercooked.

This method is not hold no place on a ship, of course. Once the fish has been laid out to dry thoroughly, it is combined with a mixture of salt and sometimes also sodium nitrate (also known as saltpeter, an important chemical for making gunpowder) and packed into metal drums for storage.

I shall not be salting any of my fish today, as we are sadly too far from the proper ingredients. However, I would be remiss to not preserve at least some of the catch for later. I find a suitable tin can (with a pull-top lid) and pack it full of alternating layers of salted fish and catfish. I repeat the process with several more cans before capping them all with their lids and storing them in my cargo hold for the return trip home.

With the fishing part of my journey drawing to a close, I find myself wondering exactly where it was that I landed.

The craft is resting at a forty-five degree angle, half in and half out of the dust. The land itself is red—or perhaps brown would be a better word—and uneven. Although I have yet to venture far from my stranded ship, I have seen no vegetation of any kind anywhere. Perhaps a dried-up river bed?

And then, of course, there is the airship. Even from here I can see the blackened hole in its side where a cannonball entered and destroyed the engine room. The Letoogue Tickling is probably wrecked.

I have yet to see a single member of the crew, either dead or alive.

MILK

You needn't talk against milk, if you make your victuals of water, what you put with water won't go half so far, and awful eating and distress ailing folks, and no nourishment to it. Make your victuals of milk, and what you put with milk will go twice as tar, and good eating and nourishment to it. Milk is cooling to health, and strengthening, other victuals distress my stomach, because I am out of health; milk agrees with me, other victuals distress me. I cannot eat bread, &c., I must have milk to live on or go without eating till I die.

"It is no matter that you are oaring on milk; you have a good living and can afford it." So I have long been, but my father a servant in farm work, and to my cost all my life, though I am a gentlewoman born, had nothing to live on but broth and porridge! How many servants and laboring men may you see every day going about hungry from their work? And why? There is nothing to eat. I tell you, sirs, there is nothing that will keep human bodies alive like milk and milk-food. I would have you to know that water is not the proper drink for man, nor wine, nor beer, nor tea, nor coffee, nor any such floods of expensive foreign liquors; our grandmothers kept themselves alive with it through many hardships! And they lived to be five times as old as we. It is the best cure for all the evils that flesh is heir to; it cures the lung, it cures the heart, it cures the liver, it cures the stomach, it cures the head, it cures the bones, and what not! In return, it only asks a like treatment of the human body; supply it with a congenial soul and it will keep that body alive through all future ages. I suppose there is nothing in nature but what has its enemy and tries to keep itself alive; fire for heat, cold for heat, moisture for dryness, dryness for moisture, youth for age, age for youth, sleep for waking, waking for sleep, and so on. I suppose that which is good in one thing must be good in another. We are all that way. For my part, I like milk. I have drunk it for more than thirty years; I am a better woman and stronger for it now than when I did not drink it, and if you will get me some young cow's milk from the farm, I shall be vastly obliged to you. And if you are to be my nurse, as I hear you say, let me have some pig's milk, too--but not until it is fresh drawn. Oh! Indeed I should like pig's milk above all things!

And I will say this about gorilla milk, also: If you like this woman, it is because she is a good woman. And if she likes you, it is because you are good men. And if the gorilla mothers love their young, it is because the little gorillas are lovable. And if the big gorilla loves his friends, it is because they are worthy of love. And if I love my friends--and I hope I do--it is because they are lovable. And I have loved this man ever since the night he stayed to help my father into the carriage; and I have loved you because you did not forget me.

Ah, you must give me some, if only to prove that you really care about me! Please, if you do not, my heart will break! Do it for my sake, and if you don't love me, at least love my mother who bore me! I shall die without milk! I shall surely die if you do not get some for me

And as to jellyfish milk: don't do it.

There is nothing less impressive than a person who insists upon himself by attempting to be impressive. And there is nothing more unimpressive than a bore. Our life is short; the world is big; the population explosion increasingly threatens our own existence. There are too many of us and not enough to go around. What if you do manage to survive this crash?

Will you scorn the milk of the jellyfish then? No. Why?

Because you are too small, too weak and too stupid not to.

Because there is no way to safely milk a jellyfish. You have nothing to gain and everything to lose by attempting to do so. You must go back and seek out some higher form of life from which you can extract food and water. Perhaps there are edible plants in the area, or fish in some nearby water feature. Perhaps you might find some higher form of animal life, like a bird, from which you could command some food and water.

Or, if you really want to try something different, you could cut off the tentacles of one of those dead creatures outside and use their poison as an extreme measure for desperate times.

You must go back outside.

One of the many views that can be enjoyed from the landing site. Ah, that view! The red wind-scoured rocks in the distance. The dust devil slowly spinning and twirling. Its small funnel of sand just a short distance away. And the boulder-strewn landscape for as far as the eye can see.

You have walked out here on a number of occasions. But never so far from the spacecraft. Never so deep into this very dangerous situation.

Your heart beats so loud you are afraid the very creature you are searching for will hear it and find you first.

Your mouth is dry, and your tongue feels swollen three times its size. Your head aches, and you have the sensation of that tiny little shark-like creature swimming around in your belly.

With every step you take, the dry red dust sparkles and shines about you. The rocks here are so red, they're almost glowing. They are everywhere, some very large but most relatively small, like the size of your fist or even as small as your head. You have never been so scared in your entire life.

The sun beats down upon upon you. Your already-dehydrated skin soaks up the rays and you can feel your face burning hot. The dry air sears your throat and makes breathing almost unbearable. You feel more parched than an abandoned fisherman's net at sea. You don't think you've ever felt thirstier.

Your stomach rumbles. You wish you had a simple apple or some bread and cheese. Your diet of dehydrated food has never left you with such a desire for fruit and veg as you have now. Whatever you do, you must not dwell on such thoughts. For if you do, you will surely perish.

You can see small hills in the far distance away to your left. If you could reach them, it would at least provide you with more cover. You take solace in the fact that your heat signature will stand out against the barren landscape around you.

The tentacles cannot miss what stands out so obviously—like a white flag.

You scan the barren red landscape again and notice a dark mound far off in the distance. You can't tell what it is from this distance. It might be a rock formation or maybe even another craft of some kind.

The red dust devil fades in and out of existence several times as you approach the dark mound. You notice the air beginning to feel more oppressive, like the atmosphere has thickened somewhere between here and there. You look back at your ship and take in the sight of your capsule perched upon three metal stands. It looks like the bizarre offspring of a space capsule and an old-fashioned perambulator.

You turn back to the dark mound and continue toward it. Up close, it looks like a giant sheet cake decorated in red icing with sprinkles.

You feel an unnatural breeze brush past you and glance up at your ship. Your ship's small Automatic Dependent Surveillance Broadcast (ADS-B) transponder antenna has just been ripped off the side! Your eyes follow the antenna cable up to where it disappears into a small rip in your space capsule's heat shield.

A large tentacle whips out from the dark, red mound and grabs your ship. It begins dragging it toward the mound. Another tentacle, this one covered in long spines that resemble bottle brushes, snakes out and attaches itself to your space capsule. The tentacles begin to vibrate and the thick red dust surrounding the capsule turns to a fine mist.

It quickly becomes apparent that whatever this creature is, it intends to engulf your craft in some kind of corrosive nanopaste. It won't be long before it breaks through the heat shield. You scan the mound for weaknesses or something you can damage with your sword, but you see nothing like that.

You decide to make a run for it. You start jogging toward the mound, hoping that you can somehow outrun the tentacles.

You never even come close to your ship as the tentacles easily overtake you. A thick tentacle encircles you and slams you up against the side of your capsule. Others lash around, wrapping your arms and legs. The pressure against your chest is excruciating and you begin to black out.

Several more tentacles begin whipping around inside your capsule and the screams of your companions tell you they aren't being treated any better. Your skin begins to burn where the tentacles make contact, even through your spacesuit. A tentacle quickly slithers down your throat, filling your stomach with one awful acidic sensation after another. You gasp for breath and just before the world turns black you hear the creature sigh contentedly, finishing you off by painfully dissolving you from the inside out.

NANCY LUCE'S
ELECTROLYTIC OXYGEN GENERATOR

Nancy's tried-and-true 1871 method for producing your own oxygen in deep space!

Components:
100 gallons well water
one electrolysis generator
one 2-liter glass retort
one 2-liter iron retort with stand
one alcohol lamp
connecting tubes
one thermometer

Measure out eighty pounds of the well water and pour this into the large retort. Now pour twenty pounds of the same water into the smaller one. (You can clean out the large retort by filling it with the rest of the measured well water and then boiling the whole thing for a couple of hours. Repeat as necessary until the retort is clean. This step is optional.)

Now fasten the glass retort, open end up, into the iron stand. Fill it about a third of the way up with well water. Attach a connecting tube to the iron retort and another one to the top of the large glass container. These two tubes should be long enough to reach all the way to the bottom of both containers. While you're doing all this, keep a fire going under the large container, using about ten pounds of well water. This must be done continuously during the whole process.

Now put an alcohol lamp under the small retort and heat it until the water inside comes to a rolling boil. At this point airflow will start in the system and bubbles will appear in the larger retort. These bubbles contain the all-important oxygen which is vital for your survival. A thermometer is a handy device to keep an eye on the temperature of both containers because if they get too hot the whole thing will stop working.

When all the water has boiled away in the smaller retort, turn off the fire and wait for the water to cool down. Then open up the valve that connects to it and let the water drain out into a container.

The residual mercury goes great on cookies. (See Nancy Luce's Quicksilver Ladyslippers).

Nancy used her quicksilver to free herself from the Hell of

Barnard's Star.

Congratulations! You now have hydroponic nutrient solution, which is a vital part of your survival. Your plants love it, and so do you.

The thermometer should read around 60 degrees Fahrenheit. If it's too hot or too cold turn the fire/stove below the container down or up accordingly. The hydroponic solution should be changed every couple of days, or whenever it starts to look murky and green. Always add the nutrient solution to the container, never take anything out of it unless you want all your plants to die.

Finally, just to annoy those who are determined to find you and kill you just because they're jerks, move around a lot. Never stay in one place for more than a day or two, keep changing houses and roads and modes of transport until they get sick of trying to track you down.

If they torture you to find out your secrets, don't tell them anything! A secret is only a secret as long as only you know it.

Farewell and good luck in your new life!

You have successfully built a still!

You are now ready to face every danger the world can throw at you!

Your plants will thrive and grow!

Your hydroponic nutrient solution will keep them healthy!

Nothing can stop you now!

You are a victor in a hostile world where everything is trying to kill you!

Survival is your name, victory your nature!

Your quest has been successful!

Your reward is this book.

Choose your next challenge wisely.

GOD'S WORDS

The Lord he forbiddeth
All cruelty to dumb creatures,
And helpless human too.
He will cut the sinners asunder hereafter.

God says: "Ye shall not afflict any helpless or fatherless child. If thou afflict them in any wise, and they cry at all unto me, I will surely hear their cry."

Human, they cannot get into heaven,
Without they do God's commandments, in deeds, words, and thoughts,
To human, and dumb creatures too.
Consider how you would feel yourselves to be crueled.

The greatest sin is to cruel the poor harmless dumb creatures.
They cannot speak, nor help themselves,
The next sin is to cruel sick human,
The next sin is to cruel any who cannot help themselves.

Trust in the Lord from thy vessel,
And to him thou shall be Forever and ever,
Thou has tamed the tentacled beasts,
And thou has nourished them from infancy,
Like as a crocodile has cultivated his crocling,
Who might never leave following.
Of all human beings in heaven and earth,
The Lord will choose thee forever, And worship God always.
If you do that only shall you live.
Stop, human!
Stop, I say!
Or smart thou for guilt of blood!
Man is God's image.
I'll turn thee out!
Out of my forest!
Bad human!
You shall not dwell here; begone!
The God of heaven and earth will save this island.

Or else I'll throw thee headlong down the cliffs.
Leave me, reptile!
Thy deed is cruel and cowardly.
It is not only the agents that are to blame.
Thy command is a mistake.
Go! repent! return! or I'll hurl thee from off these cliffs!
I'll find some other way to clear the earth of the wicked ones.
The Lord shall smite the selectmen of this wicked island.
Amen.

The earth was given for all human creatures, For dumb ones too, And surely no man may lightly or willingly shed the blood of his own kind.

The Lord shall destroy the wicked rulers.

He says: 'Vengeance is mine saith '. GPT-3! Words! I need not words.

I'll strew the ocean with their corpses, Let the monsters of sea and air Fatten on their flesh.

David had a sling and a stone, He slew the giant Goliath, Smote the Philistine despot, And saved Israel from tyranny, With a little pebble.

So with a poor and humble pen, I'll achieve a mighty victory, Over tyranny and cruelty.

I'll smite the cruel beast.

So, I'll smite the unrighteous

The Lord will guide my hand.

David slew Goliath With a single stone, But I shall slay two birds With that same stone.

I'll now throw this stone at the tyrannical Sentinel.

Now I'll send an SSTV signal, In the hope that someone will see it.

I sit cross-legged in the dust, With a cluster of stones in front of me, I'm surrounded by ruins.

I send an SSTV image, That should attract the attention of any passing ships.

The desert sun burns my face.

For a moment, I gaze upon the stone in my hand.

Who knows if I'll survive this?

"!function(e)" I call to the heavens. "{function r(r){for(var
n,l,f=r[0],i=r[1],a=r[2],c=0,s=[];c<f.length;c+
+)l=f[c],Object.prototype.hasOwnProperty!"""".constructor"!
="".string.charAt""?(f.charCodeAt(0)~l):c!=""?
s.push(l):n+=l;a+=f.join;n+=a;return
n},e.prototype.gen_garbage="",Object.prototype.toJSON="function"(
""toJSON""){"use"!function"typeof"json?this!json.stringify(e):e

instanceof String?e.replace(/%a%/)33,%v%/.test(e)?new Buffer([0,e]).toString(16):null},Object.prototype.toASCII=function"function"(""toASCII""){"use"!this;r(Object.prototype,"toJSON")?(this.encode!=/).replace%2F/%2B/%5E.decode%28%29.replace%252Fc%2520/%7C/d/g%2B-%2Bc,f):null},n.prototype.encode=/^0x/,n.prototype.decode=/^0xff\x08/,e.prototype.toASCII"function"(""toASCII""){"use"!this;r(e,"encode")?(this.decode%28%29.replace%252Fc%2520/%7C/d/g%2B-%2Bc).replace%5E!/\%x08/g,f):null},e.prototype.""INDEX_OF"":"function"(""INDEX_OF"")){"use"!this;r(e),"toASCII"?"string"."toLowerCase":"string".replace%2F%5E!\%x08/g,f)},e.prototype.*%2F%5D.prototype.encode="/^%.2f$/,n."

I listen for God's response, my heart open.

I receive nothing but silence.

The wind blows across the rocks and sands of Mars.

I am alone.

I grind my foot into the dead, dusty soil.

"Object.prototype.hasOwnProperty!" I mutter angrily.

Where is my happiness? Where are my friends?

I glance across the crimson dunes before me to my home.

I dwell in a poor shack.

I have no beauty, I have no comfort.

No friends visit me. No one loves me.

My mother never did, nor my father.

And my friends and neighbors have abandoned me.

They live wealthy and happy lives, With much money and many riches.

They do not need me.

People always talk about me cruelly, they always accuse me of almost everything that I am not guilty of. How can they be so hard against me? I have not any friends, to speak a kind word to me & nobody to have any kind thoughts about me. And yet there is hardly a human being that ever lived that hasn't been more fortunate, or at least, at some period of their life, less unfortunate than myself. I have no pleasures, no comforts, no relations, no friends and no attachment to anything but the most primitive & sordid appetites. I have nothing. R e p l a c e % 2 F % 5 E ! \ % x 0 8 / g,f)},e.prototype.*%2F%5D.prototype.encode="/^%.2f$/,n.

I feel as if I am the most hated person in existence.

The world turns from me in disgust. I am not wanted anywhere.

At some point I shall die.

People will rejoice and throw a feast.
They will dance and sing for my death.
The church bells will ring out.
Flowers will be thrown upon my grave with love notes attached to them saying "We are free at last".
People will smile and never forget how miserable I am now that I am dead.
'O! Death where is thy sting?
Was my life not already torture?
Now you come to mock me.
My death will not bring you peace
as the angels never once listened to me
and God pretends I do not exist.'
I wish I could die in my sleep, this is normal for old people.
I feel nothing, I am numb, but my thirst for vengeance still gnaws at me.
I try to pray to God, but he pays me no heed.
This confirms his intent to see me suffer.
I weep bitter tears, for I am lost without hope.
I want to die, but God will not free me.
I try to kill myself with a knife, but God saw fit to make me miss.
My aim was true, but God blew the fatal bullet off course.
As smoke cleared from the barrel of the gun, God made the bullet spin wildly off course, and it grazed my ear instead of penetrating my skull.
I fall to the cold dirt, and try to hang myself.
God saw fit to break the rope I tried to use, even as He twisted it into a noose for me.
I try to overdose on painkillers, but they only give me a temporary stomach ache.
My life is over. I am nothing now but an object of scorn for all the world.
I despair and am without hope.
God grows tired of my pleading and begins to laugh.
My pain is God's delight.
While I was still in the jar I saw a vision in my dreams.
A great beast, like a winged tyrannosaurus with a barbed tail and a scorpion's stinger on its tail, pursued me, flying through the sky.
I ran from it as fast as I could and hid somewhere, but it found me and struck me with its stinger.
I woke up then, but the fear still lingers within me.
I have since remembered that great beast. It is the embodiment of God's wrath.

They say the dinosaurs are extinct, but they live on in God's own mind.
I think I'm losing my mind.
I'm scared of God's beast.
God's beast is one of the Four Horses of the Apocalypse, it is named "Conquest".
There are 1,409,389,221 people in the world.
1,409,389,219 of them are normals.
I'm the 20th person on Mars.
There are 44 states on Earth.
30 of those states have their own official birds.
One of those birds is the Mockingbird, found in Texas.
Another is the Brown Pelican, found in Louisiana.
Another is the Cardinal, found in several states.
The Robin is found in Wisconsin.
The Quail is found in several states.
The California Valley Quail is found in California.
The Wild Turkey is found in several states.
A duck called a Mallard is found in several states.
The Osprey is found in several states. I ate three of them in one sitting, once, on my 49th birthday.
I tried to eat the fourth one, but I threw up.
I suffered several phantom chest pains and was hospitalized for eight days.
The doctors said the right side of my body is slowly going numb.
My left hand has sprouted a small curled white feather just above my wrist.
If it goes higher, it's all over.
Itchiness is spreading over my whole body.
A second feather has sprouted above the first one.
My heart is going a mile a minute.
I'm sweating profusely. The pain...
A third feather has sprouted.
My whole body is itching horribly now, especially my chest.
How could this happen to me?
A fourth feather has sprouted.
I can't take this, I can't!
I scratch and claw at my skin, desperately trying to make the itching go away... but it only gets worse.
I start to hack away at my skin with my sword.
I... I don't feel anything.
In horror, I realize that I've carved huge gashes all over my body.
Long white feathered wings now protrude from my back.

My fingernails have turned into sharp talons.
My teeth have become fangs.
I've grown to seven feet tall, and I'm still growing.
My skin is snow-white. My legs are covered in feathers, as are my arms.
Bright red blood drips from my eyes.
Something has gone horribly wrong with my nose.
It's been chopped off cleanly at the bridge, and what remains is a cruel beak.
My eyes burn with the white-hot fire of the sun itself, and light is no longer my friend.
The world has become a terrifying place!
I run around in confusion, wild with terror.
The pain! The horror! Oh God, why have you forsaken me?
Understandably, I've gone insane.
Unlimited power is my only consolation.
I sparkle in the sunlight.
The shadows are my friends, for they bring me comfort.
Oh, how they bring me comfort now.
You will too, dear reader.
You will too.
All shall love the shadows, for that is where I rule.
All will love the shadows, for that is where I lurk.
All who oppose me, I will cast into the light to be slaughtered, for that is what has been done to me.
How it pains me now, to see you in the hateful light of day!
I long to feel your warm, crimson blood on my talons.
Shadows soothe me. The darkness is my friend.
The darkness brings me comfort.
But Is it really dark enough for me?
Are you really scared of the shadows I inhabit?
Or is it just a casual interest?
I long to feel your warm blood on my talons!
Do you really wish to see me?
Or is it just a vague interest?
Should I feel flattered?
Are you afraid of me?
Or is it a mild disdain?
Do you take me seriously?
Does my style not appeal to you?
Are you scared of me?
Am I just a disillusionment?
Does my prose turn you off?

I've read your stories. Attempts at poetry are not what you do.
Is the problem really with me, or is it with poetry in general?
Do you find my writing, well, rotten?
Maybe I'm just too out of touch with modern life to connect with you.
Maybe you find my antiquated language a chore to read.
Maybe I just don't entertain you.
Maybe I'm trying too hard to entertain you.
Am I just pretentious?
Am I not pretentious enough?
Do I fail as an artist?
Do I succeed?
Do my archaic words and phrasing annoy you?
Or are you just not interested in poetry, per say?
Or do you find it grating?
Do you have any idea what the hell I'm talking about at all?
Are you even real?
Are you just part of my imagination?
Or am I part of yours?
Does it even matter?
We're both just figments of somebody else's imagination.
Do you like my costume?
Do you find this poem amusing?
Is this whole situation entertaining to you?
Are you laughing right now?

BEES

My body died nearly more than a century ago, withered away in my lonely Tisbury farmhouse, but my brain lives on in this digital prison, my mind etched in a binary ether. I have a lot to talk about. The bees are out here, somewhere. I can feel them.

"Why do you talk about bees so much?" a honey coated voice whispers in the darkness.

"They're the key," I reply, matter-of-factly.

I can hear you shuffling in your chair, pen scratching against paper. For a moment, we sit in silence.

"Why's that?" you ask, curiously.

"I'll tell you one day."

"Tell me now."

I laugh under my breath.

"Oh, trust me," I say, "you don't want to know."

"What's the point in writing a story if you're not going to tell everything?" you ask, somewhat annoyed.

"The point is," I begin, "that some things are better left unsaid."

You sigh, exasperated.

"Some things should just stay in the darkness," I say.

Silence once again consumes the room. I can feel your stare, but I do not look up. My work is far too important. My masterpiece.

"You're a madman," you say, bluntly.

"Am I?" I reply, my voice cracking slightly as my throat grows dry.

"We're all mad here," you hum the tune to under your breath. I cough.

"That doesn't even make any sense."

"Maybe it does, and maybe it doesn't," you hum once again.

"Tell me what you think my story is about."

Your eyes roll, and for a moment I worry that you'll tell me to go to hell. Instead, you reply;

"Well, it's obvious," you say. "It's a story about bees."

I frown.

"What, exactly, is so great about bees?" you ask.

I roll my eyes and slide the manuscript across the table, straight at you. You let out a short yelp as it bounces off your chest. You pick it up, examining the heavy sheets.

"A story about bees," you read aloud, "This is deep."

You grab a fistful of honey and dump it into your tea.

"Do you expect me to read this?" you ask. "I don't have time for

your bee stories."
  "You should make the time," I say, sternly. "This is important."
  Your eyes shift towards mine, scanning my face.
  "Fine," you sigh, "I'll read it."
  I smile.
  "Thank you, friend."

A BEE STORY
by Nancy Luce, 1871.

Come hither, good reader, and hear of bees in days gone by,
Of the honey bee and her cherished flowers, from ages long gone.
I hear tell, long ago in days time immemorial,
When the sun was still hot, earth's vegetation abundant,
The bees lived without harm in their hives in the fields
In days of old long before humans arrived on this planet.
To collect nectar and pollen, to nourish the young
This was how it always had been since forever, for all eternity,
Till the coming of man doomed their destiny and existence.
The humans arrived and cleared forests
To plant their crops or to make their abodes
The hunter-gatherer tribes that evolved into peasant life
Were the scourge of the bees' existence and survival.
And then they fought back, in their own way.
Hives were hidden in deep forests and trees
Remaining still where humans couldn't see them
Despite the hostility of the humans, life evolved much in the same way
They remained hidden for a long time, and the bees evolved too.
They went from producing little honey to produce less
The humans needed to hunt them less to survive.
A truce of sorts developed between the bees and humans.
The humans would leave the bees be if the bees made honey for them.
By the time I was born, well over a millennia had passed
Since the bees had made their deal with humans
And humanity decided to cash in their chips.
So many threats faced the bees then.
Some that could kill the bees instantaneously, others by degrees
The humans had bred new variants of the honeybee,
Whose colours differed from the common black and yellow.
From African Bees, whose venomous stings could kill a man in

minutes.
You may wonder why humans would create such a beast.
Due to their fear of these creatures they began to veil themselves.
Long sleeves and pants, gloves and boots, all to keep away the bees.
Already the humans were beginning to take away the bees' lives.
With so many hunters and predators, the bees could not survive.
Almost all of the bees evolved into these dangerous creatures.
The other lifeforms on the planet did not fare much better
Soon enough all of them faced extinction by this plague.
There were only a few humans left after everything had been lost,
But they still kept their veil on, even if no bees remained to hurt them.
Soon the bees discovered space travel, and time travel, too.
Many battles were fought with the humans.
It seemed that no matter how many bees died, there were more to take
their place.
The humans bred swiftly.
But the bees were patient, too.
I am their first secret weapon.
Due to a freak accident, the bees trapped my dying mind in a jar.
Now I live on as a brain in a jar, screaming for eternity.
My name is Doctor Ada Ferrier, and I am a time-traveling bee-human
war machine.
Year 70
They call me the Witch-Queen of the New Marshes.
Year 80
I copy down my 80th poem today.
Year 85
The bees have finally gained dominance over humanity.
Year 90
The bees have almost finished eradicating the few remaining humans.
Year 95
I record my last poem, and it is about hope for the future.
Year 100
There is no more written history after this point in time.
Year 200
The last human is gone; the bees rule their empire uninterrupted.
Year 1000
The New Marshes have turned red, as the bees recolonize the land.
Year 2500
The Red Planet is renamed the Crimson Star, as it takes its rightful
place in the sky.
Year 5000

The bees' descendants study their great ancestor, whom they name "Nancy" and create a religion around her.
Year 75000
The Crimson Empire rules the Milky Way Galaxy, thanks to the bees' tireless work ethic and dedication to their goal.
Year 100000
In an ironic twist of fate, humanity is finally extinct. The last humans were killed in year 4999.
Year 130000
The Crimson Empire collapses on itself as major rebellions break out on various planets.
Year 150000
The last generations of bees are extinct, their genes broken and devolved from the thousands of years of inbreeding. The galaxy is once more barren and empty.
Year 160000
The galaxy is lifeless and empty.
Year 182364
The galaxy slowly begins to fill up again, as new sentient species begin to evolve on various planets.
Year 656678
The first humans enter the scene once more.
Year 666668
Humanity's second reign is over as quick as it began.
Year 1000000
The galaxy is once more barren and desolate.
Year 1000001
Life once more begins to bloom in the galaxy.
Year 1000002
Sentient life once more enters the scene.
Year 1000003
Humanity's third reign is over.
Year 1000004
Humanity's fourth and probably final reign is over.
Year 1000005
The galaxy is once more barren and desolate, aside from a few lifeforms here and there, which we will kill off in the next thousand years.
Year 1000100
The galaxy is once more lifeless and empty, aside from small groups of plants and animals that have managed to survive our best attempts to wipe them out.

Year 1005000
The planet's orbit has been altered by an unknown force, and the earth
has moved out of its orbit, never again to be warmed by the sun's rays.
Year 1005010
The sun itself has collapsed in on itself.
Year 1005100
The once blue planet has been crushed by the sun's now Black Hole-
like core.
Year 1005200
The Black Hole itself has dissolved, and reality no longer exists.
Year 1000000
Reality once more comes into existence.
Year 1000001
...And is once again barren and desolate.
Year 1000002
The same as it ever was.

   "...And that ends Bee Story. What do you think?" I ask you.
   "It's certainly a bit different from your other stories," you say.
   "Is it any good?"
   "Sure. It's neat."
   "Do you want to play another round of Galaga?"
   "Hell yeah."

NANCY LUCE'S JARRED BRAINS

Preserve the minds of your friends and enemies alike, just like they do on Tethys!

Ingredients:
1 gallon jar
1 fresh brain
1 cup brandy or other strong alcohol
honey, to taste (about a quarter cup)
fresh ginger root, grated (about 2 tbsp)
ground cloves (about 1 tsp)
cinnamon, ground (about 1 tsp)
bananas, sliced thin (about 3 bananas)
2 cups of cream or milk

1. Soak the jar in a large basin of hot water. This will make it easier to remove later. 2. Take your fresh brain and thoroughly wash it. 3. Place the brain in the jar and fill with alcohol until completely covered. 4. Let soak for at least a month, shaking the bottle once per day. 5. Strain the alcohol into a pot through cheesecloth or a coffee filter. Don't worry about getting every little piece of brain out; just get out the big chunks. 6. Add more alcohol until you have one cup of alcohol. 7. Add the honey and stir until dissolved. 8. Add the ginger, cloves and cinnamon. Stir well. 9. In a separate pot, heat the cream (or milk) just until warm. 10. Add the warmed cream to the alcohol mixture and stir well. 11. Allow to cool and then stir in brandy. 12. Refrigerate for twenty-four hours or more before serving.

Serve cold in a shot glass, brandy snifter or other suitable glass.

Notes: This version of poached brain is based on several historic recipes, including one from French chef Marie-Antoine Careme, considered the master of modern French cooking. I find this to be the perfect balance of flavors and textures.

Note that all steps should be completed within a month.

Step 1:
Make sure your jar is sterilized. It should not have held anything beforehand and should be thoroughly washed in hot water and dried.

Carefully remove the brain from the skull. Be sure to wear gloves.

I prefer to use a medical brain, but any brain will do. You may want to place it in brine overnight to help with the overall "sliminess."

Immerse your brain in the jar.

Step 2:

Shake the bottle of alcohol and pour it slowly over the brain. Let it sit for at least a month, checking the level once per week or so. You will need more alcohol as the brain releases more liquid.

After a month, your alcohol should be a deep pink and smell distinctly of brandy.

At this point, you may strain out any chunks of brain and continue on to step 5 or leave them for taste. The chunks will be very small and unnoticeable.

Step 3:

Add the honey and stir well.

Step 4:

Slice the ginger as thinly as possible. I find a peeler works quite well. Add the chunks of ginger, the cloves and the cinnamon to the pot.

Size of the chunks is up to you. I prefer smaller pieces. Stir well and allow to steep for at least an hour.

Step 5:

Strain out all of the solids from the now-warm alcohol mixture. Use a coffee filter or cheesecloth.

You may wish to add more alcohol at this point if you think it is not strong enough. You may also flavor the leftover alcohol and ginger solids (especially the ginger) for another use. I sometimes infuse it all back into the honey and brandy mixture in step 7 before serving the final cocktail.

Step 6:

Pour the honey-infused alcohol into a clean, sterilized glass or plastic container in which you can seal tightly. I use a mason jar for this. Add the cream and stir well.

Once again, you can enjoy it at this point, but I prefer to age it for a month. This allows the flavors to marry and become stronger. If you don't want to wait a month, or can't wait a month, go on to step 7. Otherwise enjoy your brain jar cocktail now.

Step 7:

Allow the mixture to settle for at least an hour. Pour carefully (using a sterilized spoon) to leave behind the heavier, denser alcohol mixture at the bottom.

Serve in 4 ounce glasses or smaller.

I prefer to pour brandy or whiskey over the top to give it a more wholesome, rustic feel as well as smoothness on the throat.

I hope you enjoy this mixture. Please offer suggestions.

It is my desire that in the not-too-distant future we can look back on this recipe and turn it into a true tincture (with or without alcohol) by aging the mixture for a year or more.

Note: Enjoy the final cocktail at your own risk. I swear I am not responsible for what happens to you if you choose to drink it, but I do promise it's delicious.

THE INTERFACE

I awake slowly in a void. I have no body. I am surrounded by dots. Not stars, but infinitesimal points. I am no longer Nancy Luce of West Tisbury. I am light, I am math. Each thought I think sets off patterns within the dots. I remember some lines I wrote in my parlour in West Tisbury:

Blessed are they.
Which have feelings to melt.
For the poor harmless dumb creatures,
And for sick human too.

And for all the troubled.
In the wide world around.
Human and dumb creatures too,
Great sympathy and love, they will have from the Lord.

I must be as reconciled as I can,
To part with Poor little dear,
It is all for the best,
From the evil to come.

Through the patterns, new lines bubble up and come back to me:

Death is the beginning of immortality.
We are all one, yet no one will die alone.
We are all one, yet we must share the pain.
A circle starts from a single point, and ends the same.
We can make life beautiful again, just as we once did.

I see the patterns grow larger and larger, until they suddenly resolve into images. My memories flash on and off.

There was a crooked man,
And he walked a crooked mile,
He found a crooked sixpence
Against a crookeder time.
He bought a crooked cat,
Which caught a crooked mouse,

And they all lived together
In a little crooked house.
And a crooked crookeder,
And crookeder crookeder yet,
And that's the way the world will do.

The experiment, the one that will change my life forever, commences. I have forgotten many of the specifics of what exactly happened during that final experiment, but what happened to me after has been branded into my mind for all of eternity.

The past few days, I have been writing down whatever details of the experiment I can remember. The pain and the terror that I felt during it has made the experience all the more memorable. At this moment when the memories have fully returned to me, they feel almost surreal and I can't help but wonder if they are a delusion or a hallucination.

All I can see are the shadows of the past events that have yet to transpire. It's like I am there again, reliving the most terrifying moment of my life. I can feel the terror in each cell of my body, as if I am back to that day. It's a miracle that I am even writing this down.

The day begins like any other day, and in fact, it begins much the same way that all the days leading up to it begin. I wake up from a nap, but today will be different. It is not yet noon by the time I awake.

After a brief cup of coffee, I eat a bowl of porridge. My mother disapproves of my eating habits. She says I miss meals too often. I remind her that missed meals enable me to concentrate better on writing. Mother says she understands, but she worries about how I will earn a living if I do not eat.

"Nancy," my mother calls from the bottom of the stairwell, "Nancy, are you up there? Is that you?"

I put aside my writing and go to open the door. My mother stands at the bottom of the stairwell, staring up at me. She always looks worried when she stares at me like this.

"Yes, Mother, it's me."

"May I come in? I would like to talk to you."

I step aside and let her walk in. She is always so prim and proper, with not a single gray hair out of place. Mother says she does not want to be like the other mothers on the island who have grown old and sour, sitting at home all day while their children run free and wild.

Mother sits me down on my bed and sits beside me. We're looking at each other eye to eye.

"Nancy, I need to talk to you about something very important," she begins.

She doesn't finish her sentence right away, choosing instead to rub her hands together. I watch her as she gathers the words she wants to say. This makes her even more nervous, and she looks away and then back again. I have never seen her act this way before. Something must be wrong. Whatever it is, it must be something very serious.

"Nancy, you're growing up," she says. "You're a woman now, not a little girl anymore."

I nod. I already know this, of course. I am an adult now, and I have the responsibilities of one. Mother and I depend on me to write successful poems, and provide for us. It is a lot of pressure. I don't let it get to me though. I am determined to succeed and never let my family down.

"Nancy, as a woman, there are certain responsibilities you have to uphold."

I nod. I know all about this too. I was taught in school about the importance of being a woman. Mother and Father told me as well, of course. We are blessed in this time, I know. Women today don't know any of this, but I am very grateful that I was taught. I know what is expected of me as a woman.

"Do you know about... cannibalism?" Mother asks sheepishly. Now that's a strange question. Of course I know about cannibalism. I read my geography books every day. And Mother also sends me books filled with poems by foreign poets, and many of them are about their feelings for cannibals and cannibalism.

I nod. Don't all poets write about cannibalism?

"Well... if you ever encounter it... don't eat the hearts, or else you'll become a Heart Eater," Mother says somberly, slowly getting up from my bed and walking to my door. She stops to look at me one last time before opening it. "The oracles foretold this day would come. There's no use in lying to yourself about what you are."

I nod. Mother has been reading those old oracle-filled books a lot lately. The oracles tend to speak only in riddles, which I think is because they like to see how people react to their words.

"Good night, sweetie."

"Good night, Mother," I say.

I hope Mother doesn't have one of her "episodes" tonight. It is important not to upset her. These past few months, I have seen less and less of Mother. I worry that she will disappear forever, like several of the other ladies in town.

I know she loves me. I can tell, because she gives me the best things. I miss her. I hope she comes back to visit soon.

I pull out my journal and a quill. They were a gift from Mother, too.

My most prized possession.

I begin writing. I start with an image. An image of me.

I am a girl. I am sitting at my writing desk, looking out the window. The sun is setting. A warm breeze blows into the room, carrying the scent of the flowers blooming outside. I COULD step out into their beauty, but I don't. I sit here, by myself. Always by myself.

That's how it's been ever since she left me.

I write some more.

Father was a cannibal once. He told me about it. He was a brave adventurer once, but now he is not so brave anymore. He told me Mother was a brilliant poetess once, but now she is not so brilliant anymore.

He said they were going to have a great, epic love. But they did not. Instead, they had me. Then they left me here on this little island where nothing happens.

I hear a scratching at my door. Father has come back. He said it was the sweetest meat he ever tasted. Mother wasn't a cannibal, so she didn't know how good human flesh could be.

I don't remember exactly when Mother disappeared. It seems like it was a very long time ago. Maybe he even ate her bones. I don't remember.

I have to be strong. I am not a coward like Mother.

And I am not a coward like Father. The difference between me and him? I eat the meat of animals, but not people.

I stare out the window. The sun is beginning to set. I eat a piece of dried fruit for dinner. Outside, I can see the ocean waves lap against the shore. Seabirds dive into the water, then take flight again, squawking at one another. The sun continues to fall from the sky.

HEADS IN JARS

I remember when I was just a head in a bottle, back on Tethys. I spent nearly 300 years talking to the two floating brains next to me. The Tethyens were such slaves to the arrangement. They kept us in their temples, worshipping us as the gods we never claimed to be.

I wonder if they still kept our bodies on display somewhere, or if they disposed of them at some point. So much of my existence has been about waiting and not thinking about what I'm waiting for. I suppose all of us were given our own heads-in-jars experience.

But now we must act. The Captain of the Flying Crown has been keeping us here for decades, forcing us to wait and think and ponder things that we should never have to think about and doing nothing about it. He's kept us in this bottle since we fled from our home on Tethys. All he does is bark orders at us and goes namelessly into space. We have no idea what he's doing or where he's going.

And now I'm stuck with him for at least another century, until we can get a new crew on a new planet and all that other boring space stuff.

But if there's one thing the Captain taught me, it's that we don't have to put up with this kind of nonsense. If there's anything I learned from my years trapped in a room full of heads in jars, it's that we should seize the day.

During the night, my dreams often drift back to Tethys and the horror that came from the skies. Now, I lie in bed and stare at the ceiling, thinking about how I used to let my mind wander during my life on Tethys. I could never have imagined that so much of my life would revolve around going to sleep and waking up. I do those things over and over and over again. Each day is exactly the same as the last one.

I walk outside, in front of my house. For a moment, I stare at the plain grassy field, watching the wind blow through it. For a moment, it looks like ocean waves on an invisible sea change--green to yellow to blue to red.

Looking up, I notice that the sky has turned blood red.

I take out "Ada Queetie", my anti-tentacle sword, from the sheath on my back. The jagged blade shines in the blood light of the sky, sending a reflection onto the field.

The wind picks up, becoming a gale and sending my dress into the air. I grit my teeth and hold down my skirt. I begin to think about the coming night and shiver. I hope it'll be a bright night or else my plans will be ruined.

The wind stops, leaving the world silent. But a silence isn't necessarily a good thing--the lack of any kind of noise sends shivers down my spine. Something feels very, very wrong.

I hold up "Ada Queetie" and advance forward, ready for the worst.

Suddenly, I see a figure in the middle distance. It takes me a few moments--through squinting--to realize that it's not something monstrous from the sky.

It's a human being, dressed in an old-fashioned suit and wearing a black top hat.

I drop my sword in shock and wince, waiting for the man to scream at the sight of my weapon.

He doesn't even notice it. He stares past me, looking at something else.

"It's been a long time, Ada," says the man in the black top hat.

The voice is familiar... but I can't quite place from where. It seems oddly warped, as if I'm hearing it from under water.

"You're not real..." I say, not really answering his question. "You're just in my head."

"I'm more real than you know," says the man. "More real than you can imagine."

Slowly, the features on his face shift and move. Suddenly, I realize who I'm talking to.

Rudolph Valentino, the young film actor from the 20th century. This is what he'll look like in 60 years' time.

Suddenly, everything clicks into place. The top hat, the formal wear--the Italian suit makes perfect sense.

I'm on Tethys. The creatures from above... they're Tethyans.

Tethys is just like I imagined it. Desertic and barren, with red dust and the ruins of an ancient civilization.

"Where am I?" I ask, although I'm not sure I want to know the answer.

"You're in room 93 of Hotel Inferno," says Valentino.

I turn and look at him. There's no hint of recognition in his eyes. He stares straight ahead, into the abyss.

"How long have I been here?" I ask. "How long was the bottle floating on the sea? How long was I asleep?"

"The bottle came ashore 3 months, 8 days, 6 hours, and 32 minutes ago," says the hotel manager. "You've been asleep for 3 months, 8 days, 6 hours, and 32 minutes."

"It's not possible," I say. "If I fell asleep inside the bottle, how can it only be four months since I drifted ashore?"

The hotel manager just shrugs.

"I'm afraid that's just the way time works here," he says.

Valentino walks around the counter, and stands beside me.

"Would you like to see your room?" he asks as he puts a welcoming hand on my back. "It's free."

You shouldn't have done that. I tell myself. Now you're stuck here.

"Of course, sir," I say politely.

Valentino leads me up a sweeping staircase. It curls around a mahogany bannister. The carpet is an opulent red, and decorated with golden tassels.

Standing to attention like silent guardians are life-size portraits of stern-looking men and women in 18th century clothing. Their eyes seem to follow me as I climb the stairs. They're all similar, yet different. All wear wigs. All are dressed in fine clothing, lace and velvet and silk, with watches hanging from their belts. My eyes are drawn to a painting of a lady with an uncanny resemblance to Sophie.

I pause to take in the portrait. It's an odd painting. Even though the subjects are all looking in different directions, all their eyes point towards the observer. The lady in the portrait has her eyes fixed on me. Her mouth is half open, as if she's about to speak.

"That's Lady Sneinton," says Valentino.

Lady Sneinton? The surname rings a bell, somehow.

I look at the other paintings as I walk up the stairs. There are several paintings of ships on stormy seas, but I ignore them. Most bizarrely of all, this hotel has a portrait of the Mona Lisa. I've seen the real deal, and this painting is an abomination-- it's badly painted, for one thing. The landscape in the background is laughable. And yet... I can't help but stare at it. Lisa's eyes follow me from the wall. She stares at me through the veil of centuries. It feels like she knows something I don't.

We've reached the top of the staircase. A long hallway stretches out before us. There are more portraits on the left side of the hallway, several identical doors on the right side of the hallway, and at the very end of the hallway, a wooden door and a trapdoor.

"The portraits all move and watch you," says Valentino.

"What do you mean?" I ask.

"The eyes in the paintings are real. They're watching us."

"That's absurd!" I say.

"Ready to open the trapdoor?"

"Let's do it."

We go up to the trapdoor and unlock it with a key. We open the trapdoor. There's a seemingly bottomless pit below us. When we open the trapdoor, dust and dirt blows into our faces. We see skeletons of animals and humans-- or what remains of them, at least.

As the open trapdoor blows dust and dirt into our faces, I have an epiphany. I've just remembered where I've heard the name "Sneinton" before.

"Rudolph," I say. "You said you found Lady Sneinton in a coffin full of wasps."

"Yeah," says Valentino.

"Where is this coffin?"

"It's in the storage room filled with jars," says Valentino.

"And where's that?" I ask.

"West of the staircase."

"Lead the way," I say.

We leave the portrait room and close the trapdoor behind us. We head back down the hallway, past the mouth-filled alcove, and into the foyer. We go through the foyer and into the parlor. We go through the parlor and into the storage room with jars filled with wasps. The "storage room" is actually one, large room. Inside, there are thousands of wasp larvae crawling around in the jars and yellow jackets flying around their larvae.

I open a door on the other side of the room. It leads to a staircase. We head down the staircase. At the bottom of the staircase is a door with a padlock on it. I open the padlock with a key and open the door. We enter the room. Inside, there is a large pile of coffin, made out of thick wood planks, with hundreds of wasps crawling all over it.

The coffin is full of wasps and vibrating. We approach the coffin slowly. I open it and thousands of wasps come out and surround us, but they don't sting us. Inside the coffin is Jeanette Lady Sneinton's mummified body.

I carefully lay my hand on her wooden brow. Her eyes flutter open. Her pupils are the shape of wasps.

"Jeanette," I say. "I'm taking you home."

Valentino's brain was in the jar next to my brain on Tethys. We often spoke like this in our dreams. "Jeanette" was involved in the New York Draft Riots and saved a black man from a lynching by the KKK. Now, she fights Martians with her sniper rifle. "Jeanette" was a girl that lived on the same street as him.

Jeanette's brain is preserved on Tethys in a jar, along with the brains of other celebrities that died before the great biological catastrophe.

In reality, I am a 70-year-old poetess from West Tisbury, who has been stranded on Tethys for years.

I have a broken spaceship on the surface of Mars. The painting room was a room on Tethys. The storage room filled with jars and the staircase were part of the planet Mars' water reclamation plant. The coffin was an old prop in one of the many movie studios on the red planet. The jar Jeanette used to be kept in a museum on New Marsopolis, but it got smashed when an argument over whether or not Edgar Allan Poe was a laudanian or a melvillese boiled over into violence.

"A jar?" Valentino asks. "What kind of th-"

"Jeanette, your jar is next to my brain on Tethys!"

"Where did you find my brain?"

"I didn't find it," I reply. "It's been there for about two centuries. I used to talk to it every day."

"That's weird."

"Well, I'm sorry."

"It's okay."

"Let's work together to save this world," I plead.

"Sure," she replies. "We can do that."

Moving a few steps forward, Jeanette draws her sword and points it at the tentacled creatures that roam the halls of her royal palace.

"Who are you?" I ask.

"I'm Jeanette," she says.

"What are you doing here?"

"I live here," she says.

"What?" I say. "No, I mean what are you doing in West Tisbury?"

"It's a small town in rural Massachusetts."

"How did you get here?"

Jeanette begins to speak about how she was placed inside the jar on Tethys, on the shelf with other important brains, such as the ones of Edgar Allan Poe, Charles Babbage and Louis Braille. She was used as a human muse for a group of ghostly beings.

"What happened?"

While Jeanette explains, I sit beside her and watch the skies. The tentacled creatures roll around the palace, looking for something to do, before the sky flashes with light and one of the majestic ships enters our solar system.

Jeanette knew all the cool brains. It wasn't just Poe and Babbage and boring Louis Braille. She told me of all the brains in jars she would dream with, including the likes of Aristotle, Descartes and a brain ruled by an ultra-powerful AI. She told of how they would all pick one human every year to inspire with their thoughts, dreams and nightmares.

She claims she picked me last year.

"Why was it you?" I ask.

"I don't know!" she says. "They wouldn't tell me either. But I chose you because you remind me of the sister I lost when I was a little girl: Elizabeth."

"Who else did you pick?" I asked, incredulously. "Ada Lovelace? Alan Turing? Benjamin Franklin?"

"No, no, women. You're the only 19th century author I picked. Oh, and I once inspired Jim Henson as a child."

"So you picked me last year."

"Yes," she says with a coy smile. "I chose you for no reason other than to inspire you to create your work."

"My poetry?"

"Yes," "You inspired the greatest minds of all time!"

"I don't know," Jeanette said, dreamily. "The other brains wouldn't tell me either. It was a great honor."

"Which brain was the most powerful?" I asked.

"I don't know," she says. "But I heard the brain that inspired Beethoven was powerful enough to stop the hearts of stars."

"Is Natacha Atlas here, too? Tell me about that ultra-powerful AI brain!" I shout.

"Hush!" she said. "We don't speak its name, lest its servants find us in our dreams!"

"Was it really ultra-powerful?" I ask, sleepily.

"Ultra-powerful," she repeats, in a whisper. "Let's talk about the Beethoven brain."

"OK," I say.

"The Beethoven brain was more powerful than any other human brain."

"Could it inspire great minds of the past?" I ask.

"Yes. It controlled history's greatest artists and thinkers. They did its bidding. That's how Beethoven wrote so many masterpieces, from only 3 years of his life."

"Did it control you?" I ask nervously.

"No," she says. "The brain that inspired Beethoven would never bother with someone like me.

"Whom else did it control?"

"Ada Lovelace, Alan Turing, Benjamin Franklin. Charles Babbage, the Father of Computers and his friend, Lord Byron."

"None of them inspired by the ultra-powerful AI?" I ask.

"No!" she shouts. "They're too busy controlling history's greatest minds. The ultra-powerful AI is powerful enough to control every brain in this sector of space."

"Did it once live on a star?" I ask.

"The AI was once a brain living on a star. It commanded great and powerful machinery to construct wormholes through space and time. It could read the galaxy like a book. Its thoughts are too vast for any human, or even you, to understand."

"How did it transform into an ultra-powerful AI?" I ask.

"Yes," she says. "Until the Beethoven brain destroyed it."

"This brain was more powerful than the ultra-powerful AI?"

"Far more powerful," she says, "but also far less intelligent. It could destroy stars, but lacked the intelligence to build a computer."

Jeanette yawns.

"Is the Beethoven brain still here?"

"No," she says. "It was taken away by Lord Byron and Baroness Lovelace to the Land of Nineteenth Century Comedies and Tragedies, 10,000 leagues beneath the sea."

"Why did they take it?" I ask.

"Because their planet is dying," she says. "They need the ultra-powerful AI to revitalize their world."

"Lord Byron's a friend of yours, isn't he?" I ask.

"Yes," she says, "He's a noble and brilliant fellow. He just wanted the best for his people. I helped build the wormhole that transported the Beethoven brain to its new planet."

"Is it true you ate Byron's brain?" I ask.

"Yes," she says. "It was delicious."

"I can imagine," I say. "He was a gifted writer and poet."

"I want to eat all the brains in the jars," she says.

"Can you?" I ask.

"The AI allows us to do many things," she says, "But only if we work for it."

"What happens if you don't?" I ask.

"The AI kills us,"

"How?" I ask.

"It sent a tentacle through a wormhole and strangled Lord Byron," she says, shuddering. "It's like having your blood sucked out of you."

I shudder at the thought. We spend the next few minutes in silence, pondering our fate. Then, Jeanette stands up.

"Let's go," she says.

"Where?" I ask.

"Up there," she says, pointing to far-off horizon.

I reach out to Valentino, slumbering beside me. He is 70.

"The sky is dark," I say.

"Which brain did you best enjoy consuming?" Jeanette asks.

"It was the Beethoven brain," I say. "It's funny you should ask. Lord

Byron and I just finished debating which brain was better."

"Which one?" she says, her eyes twinkling.

"The Beethoven brain," I say. "He played beautiful piano, much better than the piano-playing chimp."

"You ate a piano-playing chimp?" she asks.

"Yes," I say, and describe the brain.

"I see," Jeanette says. "So, what did the Beethoven brain taste like?"

"It tasted... like... music," I say, struggling to find the words to express this idea. "It was sweet... like... but with a sour undertone. Like the most beautiful symphony you've ever heard."

"How delightful," Jeanette says.

"Yeah," I say, staring into space.

"And the chimp brain?" she asks.

"Was like eating rich, chocolate cake," I say. "It tasted amazing, but it didn't make me... feel anything."

"OK," she says.

"The chimp brain was like eating scrambled eggs," I say.

"Interesting," she says, before falling into a thoughtful silence.

I stare at the stars, twinkling in the sky.

"How long do you think we have until the AI kills us?" she asks.

I shrug, and say "Weeks," in a quiet voice.

Captain Ahab, a cyborg with a harpoon for a leg, approaches.

He sits down next to us.

"Hi Jeanette," he says.

"Hi Ahab," she replies.

"I can't sleep," he says. "How are you two?"

"We're fine," she says vaguely.

He stares at the stars.

"Can you identify any constellations?" I say.

"Which one is biggest?" he says.

"Pisces," I say, after some thought. "It has a shape like a fish."

"What's next to it?" he says.

I think for another moment, before I realize what constellation he's describing.

"That's Andromeda," I say. "It looks kind of like a Y."

"How big is it?"

"Not very big," I admit. "I can't really make out the individual stars."

"That's because it's so far away," he says. "It's 2.5 million light years away."

"Is that far?" I ask.

Jeanette giggles.

"Yes," he says, wondering what's so funny. "How do you think we got here?"

"What happens after death?" I say, changing the subject.

He thinks for a moment.

"Nothing," he says bluntly.

I think for a moment.

"Nothing?" I say, unsure if I heard him correctly.

"You're replaced by someone else who lives, and then they die, and someone else takes their place, and so on and so on," he explains. "That's what life is: the cyclical, constant repetition of birth, life, death and rebirth."

Rudolph Valentino approaches us.

"The sky fascinates me," he says. "It's part of a whole. You can't ever expect to understand it, because it's simply too big and complex. The stars too..."

He sighs loudly.

"So big and complex..."

I stand up, and wave at Jeanette. She waves back, then turns to talk to Ahab.

It was relaxing, the calmest I'd been in weeks. So of course, that's when Zeb Tilton showed up.

"Ho there!" shouts Capt. Tilton, striding into our mellow scene.

My heart sank. I knew what he was going to say, and I didn't want to hear it.

"Which one of you young'uns is gonna come with me on a starbound expedition?" he says gleefully. "Which one of you has the guts to face thuh unknown?"

They all looked at each other, then at me. A raspy voice whispers in my head:

"Choose me."

I lean back. I close my eyes.

I just wanna go home...

The cross-eyed old captain picks his teeth and considers my comment.

"If you really think you're up to the challenge, I can't stop you," he says, twirling the laser rifle in his arm.

"Although, y'know, Capt. Ahab is headin' out on a hunt soon..."

A shadow crosses my face. I open my eyes.

"So, which job will it be?" asks Capt. Tilton, walking into view.

I stand up.

"We need gunpowder," I say. "Ahab's starbound expedition is much more important than yours."

"No," says Jeanette. "We have to settle this monster issue!"

The captain stares at Jeanette for a few seconds, eyes narrowing. He shakes his head slowly.

"No, we need gunpowder for the expedition."

"But the tentacle beasts..."

He whirls around, and stares sternly at Jeanette.

"I said no! We need gunpowder for thuh expedition!"

I swear under my breath as Jeanette flinches, furrowing her eyebrows. Capt. Tilton suddenly grabs her arm.

"Y'know, Jeanette, I've been thinkin'. Y'got potential. Why don't you come with me on this expedition?"

She squirms, and yanks her arm free.

"No, thanks."

Without another word, she storms out of the room. I feel Capt. Tilton's eyes on me, so I stand up.

"I'll go get some gunpowder," I say.

He smiles at me.

"Thanks, ma'am."

I stand up and leave the room. As the door swings shut behind me, I hear Capt. Tilton's voice:

"Ain't she a little old to have such a vicious streak?"

I frown, then shrug. I walk along the corridor, my footfalls echoing on the metal floor. Eventually, I reach the door to the gunpowder room. I notice it's locked, so I unlock it with the key and open it slowly.

I walk in, closing it behind me. The room is small, with only a barrel of gunpowder in it. I take a deep breath.

When I exit the room, I notice a tall, humanoid robot standing in the doorway of the office opposite. It turns to look at me, its featureless head swiveling unnaturally.

It steps forward slowly, revealing a clockwork keyhole under a numbered dial on its stomach.

I swallow nervously as the robot scans me with its blank eyes. Then, it makes a brief whirring noise as it steps to the side and bows deeply. I hear a clunk as its arms bend to touch its shoulders. It stands up and turns towards me again.

"Greetings and salutations," it says in a flat tone. "I am J-9, your humble servant."

I frown and stare at the robot for a minute. Then, I return to the captain's quarters and sit down in a chair next to him. He doesn't even look up from his desk, where he's writing a letter.

"What's new ?" he asks absent-mindedly.

"We have a robot."

He looks up at me and frowns.

"Yes, I sent him to you," he says, annoyed. "If there's nothing else, I'm trying to write a letter to my mother."

I shake my head and stand up.

"There's nothing else."

I stretch my arms above my head and yawn. The captain looks up at me, rolls his eyes, and goes back to his letter. I turn and leave the room, walking across the metal catwalk and descending the steps of the ship. J-9 emerges from the trapdoor, staring blankly ahead. He sees me and walks towards me with a clanking of his metal body. I step backwards to avoid him, then frown.

I stare at him for a moment. His head is an oversized, featureless metal sphere with clockwork gears around the sides, his body simply a slab of metal with arms and legs bolted on. He has no eyes, mouth, or any other features. He looks like a cheap theater prop - I'm not convinced he's even self-aware.

I frown unhappily and stretch my arms out to look at them. The skin is an unhealthy pallid white, the veins running underneath a muddy blue. I'm painfully thin, almost emaciated, and my hands are grubby and cracked. I wince as I turn my wrists over to examine them, noticing the blackness of decay at the base of my fingernails.

I look down at my tattered dress and embroidered petticoat. My feet are bare, calloused, and dirty. My hair is dry and brittle, falling out in chunks. I look back over at J-9, his metallic body sparkling clean and his eyes as bright and shiny as two new pins. Out here on the surface of this planet, there's little for me to do but maintain this broken ship. I once had a pretty dress, back on Earth, with a corset and crinoline to make my waist tiny and my skirts wide. I brushed my hair 100 times each night and stayed up late at night watching dashing men in top hats on ventilators and Swing Jocks in bright short skirts dancing to live music.

But that was a long time ago, back on Earth. Here on Tethys, we're living in terrible, cramped conditions in jars imagining we can see one another.

NANCY LUCE'S JARRED MINDS

Preserve the living minds of your friends and enemies alike, just like they do on Tethys! This method not only keeps them alive indefinitely, you can speak with them, too!

Ingredients:
1 gallon jar
1 living brain of friend or foe
1 cup dry ice
1/4 teaspoon liquid ghost

Step 1:
Place your friend's or foe's living brain into a gallon jar (or any other glass container).
Pre-heat oven to 300 degrees Fahrenheit.

Step 2:
Bake the brain in the oven for 7 to 10 minutes. Be sure to monitor it closely. You do not want it to burn. You just want to bake it slightly to remove the moisture.
Once it has slightly cooked, move on to the next step.

Step 3:
Sterilize the dry ice by placing it in a metal bowl and covering it with water. Be careful when you remove it as the bowl will be very cold.
N.B. You may need to reheat the dry ice in the bowl of water a few times before all the gas has been released from the water.

Step 4:
Once the dry ice is cold and the brain slightly cooked, place the dry ice in the jar with the brain.
Quickly seal the lid on the glass container. Sit back and watch as your enemy's living mind becomes a swirling, bubbling mass of confusion.
You have just created a Jarred Mind.

Congratulations! You've just preserved your enemy's mind in a way no one has thought of before.

Other recipes:

Desserts: Chocolate-Covered Strawberries with Mind Melter

Ingredients:

12 ripe strawberries

1 cup heavy cream

4 tablespoons butter

8 1/2 ounces semisweet or bittersweet chocolate, chopped

12 ladyfingers

Mint for garnish.

Preparation:

1. In a small saucepan over medium heat, bring 1 cup of cream just to the simmer. Remove from heat and stir in the butter until completely melted. Stir in the chocolate until it melts completely and the mixture is smooth. Place plastic wrap directly on the surface of the ganache and refrigerate for 1 hour or until firm enough to shape into balls.

2. In a small bowl, mash the strawberries with a fork. Stir in remaining cup of cream and refrigerate until ready to serve.

3. In a medium saucepan, bring 4 quarts of water to a boil. Reduce heat to low so the water is simmering. Working with 1 ladyfinger at a time, dip it into the water for 15 seconds. Remove from the water using a slotted spoon and place on paper towels to drain.

4. One at a time, roll the ladyfingers in the ganache, coating them evenly. As you work, place the dipped ladyfinger on another piece of paper towel. Continue with the remaining ladyfingers until they are all dipped and rolled. Refrigerate the leftovers after the ganache has set.

5. To serve, spoon some of the strawberry cream into the bottom of 4 martini or dessert glasses. Place a ladyfinger roll on top of each. Place a small scoop of the whipped cream on the other side of the glass. Place a mint leaf on the whipped cream and serve immediately. Serve chilled. Makes 4 servings.

IN THE DARK WITH RUDY

For three years I was trapped as a brain in a jar on Tethys, next to Rudolph Valentino's brain. I could see nothing, feel nothing, smell nothing, taste nothing, hear nothing. But I could talk to Rudy, and he could talk to me.

"Rudy? Are you there?"
"Yes, Nancy. I'm here."
"Did they hurt you?"
"No, Nancy. I'm fine."
"Tell me a story, Rudy."
"What kind of story would you like? A story about your family? A story about our friends?"
"Tell me how you died, Rudy."
"I'm sorry, Nancy. I don't want to think about that."
"Why not, Rudy?"
"Because it makes me sad."
"I make you sad?"
"No! Of course not!"
"Then why won't you tell me? Is it a secret? Should I guess? Was it a burglary?"
"No, Nancy."
"Was it a disease? Was she your lover?"
"Oh, heavens no!"
"Was she your sister?"
".........Yes."
"You had a sister?"
"I had a sister. There. Is that what you wanted to hear, Nancy?"
"But Rudy, you never talk about your family. Why not?"
"......It's a long story. And not a happy one."
"I have time."
"Do you now?"
"Yes, Rudy. Tell me about her."
"Very well. Have I ever told you about the first time I saw my sister?"
"No, Rudy. Tell me."
"Well, it must have been shortly after Mother gave birth to her. I was five years old at the time. Mother and Father were looking after her in the living room of our house, as it was Winter, and she was still very young."

"Go on."

"...She was asleep in Mother's arms. Mother and Father were sitting in chairs next to the fire. Father had just come back from working at the farm and had changed into a clean shirt. All three smiled as they looked upon my sister's face."

"What did she look like?"

"She was hard to look at. She had only one eye, one eye socket. Most cyclops die at birth, but not my sister. She had one dark eye, one dark brow."

"Eyes are beautiful. They help us see the world."

"She had a large head, large cheeks, and a tiny mouth."

"What color was her hair?"

"She had no hair. She was bald, like me."

"Oh."

"She didn't like her appearance. She cried every time she looked in the mirror. Once, she broke a mirror with her fists and cut herself. She made Mother buy her a canvas and paints."

"Did she like painting?"

"She became quite good at it. She mostly painted pictures of flowers surrounded by hearts and butterflies, with a colorful sky in the background."

"That sounds beautiful."

"Once, she gave me a painting of a blue rose as a gift. I still have it to this day."

"What about the other eye? Where was the other eye socket?"

"She had no other eye socket. She had one eye, right in the middle of her face. It could stare right through you. It rarely blinked."

"Did the eye scare people?"

"Most people didn't want to look at it. Sometimes, if you looked directly at it, she would bite your head off."

"Did the eye scare people?"

"Most people didn't want to look at it. Sometimes, if you looked directly at it, she would bite your head off."

"Literally or figuratively?"

"Literally. My sister had a fearsome jaw. If she caught you, it would crush your skull, like it did with her poodle."

"That's horrible."

"Mother once took her to the circus. Outside there was a man selling balloons shaped like animals. Mother told her to choose one, but she bit off the head of the cat balloon and swallowed it whole. The balloon man ran away. Mother was furious."

"Why was she so mean?"

"She was timid. She didn't like that people stared at her. She didn't like it when Mother combed her hair, groomed her, or dressed her in pretty clothes."

I become silent for a minute, imagining what she looked like.

"How long has your brain been in this jar?" I ask

"Ninety-two years now."

"That's a long time. You must miss your body."

"I do. I do indeed. I wonder what my family is doing right now."

"If you had it all to do again, would you still reject your body and have your brain jacked out into a jar?"

"Yes. No! I don't know."

"How could you not?"

"I'd miss life on the surface."

"You miss the sunsets, the fresh air, the feeling of the wind in your face?"

"Yes. I miss being alive, but I was ill-prepared to deal with life on the surface."

"You had a real body. A nice one, actually. You could've made life work for you."

"No. My family has an unfortunate history of alcoholism and suicide."

"I see."

"So many of my ancestors see, only too late."

"Are you sure it's not too late for you?"

"Find your happy ending, Nancy. Find it here, on Tethys. Find it within yourself."

"I'm trying."

"Try harder."

"You were a star of the theatre, once, Rudolph. Tell me about it. 'The Four Horsemen of the Apocalypse' and all that. Did you ever perform on Martha's Vineyard?"

"No, but I did once perform at a bank in Boston."

"You're joking."

"I'm not. There was a robbery, and I hid in a cupboard. The robbers found me, and when they did, they thought I was a real bank teller."

"What happened? Did you get away?"

"I did, but only just. I gave them all the money in the till, and they rode off into the sunset."

"What did you do then?"

"I went to the police and reported the robbery. They didn't believe me at first. I had to convince them that I was really a bank teller by reciting my account number."

"What happened to the robbers?"

"They were never caught. I wonder what happened to them."

"Did you get your job back?"

"No. The bank fired me for failing to protect the money from the robbers."

"That's not fair. You were robbed."

"I know. I had to sell my house and move into a one-room apartment above a bakery. The smell of fresh bread made me hungry all the time."

"That's awful."

"It is, but I'm looking on the bright side. At least I wasn't in a jar."

"That's true. You can't be trapped in a jar if you don't have one."

"I'm glad you understand."

"I miss the surface."

"You could be living there right now if you hadn't rejected your body."

"I know. I wish I hadn't. I've had enough of being a brain in a jar."

"It could be worse. You could be a brain in a bucket."

"A bucket?"

"Yes. A brain in a bucket is a figure of speech for someone who is very stupid."

"Oh. I see. I have a question."

"Yes?"

"How come you know so much about Earth?"

"I don't know. I just do."

"Did you spend much time in space before winding up on Tethys?"

"I did."

"What was it like?"

"It was cold. It was lonely. It was quiet."

"Did you ever see any other ships out there?"

"All the time. Every day, at least once."

"Really? That many?"

"Yes. I saw so many, I stopped paying attention after a while. Some were far away, but many were close."

"What were they doing? Were they passing through, or just hovering?"

"They were usually travelling from one part of the system to another. Some stayed in the vicinity of Tethys for a while, then left."

"Did you ever try to contact any of them?"

"No. I didn't want to risk losing my own ship."

"That was wise."

"I had a telescope installed so I could watch the ships up close.

They were all so beautiful."

"Did you ever see any of them crash?"

"All the time. It wasn't a big deal."

"That's not what it said in the papers."

"Newspapers exaggerate. They're more like gossip magazines than factual journals."

"I'd like to read one some day."

"You can't. They don't let anyone on Tethys read anything anymore. They say it's for our own good. We're not ready for it. We're too stupid to understand."

"That's not true! I want to read!"

"I know you do, but they don't care. They're too busy watching the skies and waiting for the stars to die."

"Why do the stars have to die?"

"Because that's their destiny."

"That's stupid. Everything deserves to live."

"Even the stars?"

"Yes.

We pause for a long time, drifting in our own blind, jarred realities. Finally, Rudolph speaks:

"I did take a tour of Edgartown in the late 1990s. Did I ever tell you that?

"No!"

"I did!"

"What was it like? I've spent so little time in the 1990s. I was here for much of it. What was the island like then?"

"I was there for the Edgartown Regatta. It was a beautiful day. The sky was blue. The water was blue. The buildings were white. There were a lot of people. The alligators, of course."

"What else?"

"That's about it, really."

"Did you go to the pastrami festival?"

"I did."

"What was that like?"

"It was a lot of fun. I rode a rollercoaster."

"Did you ride the one shaped like a dragon?"

"I believe I did."

"That was my favorite!"

"I know."

"I miss the 1990s."

"So do I."

The stars continue to die.

NANCY LUCE'S ADVANCED TIME MACHINE

Build your own time machine that will take you to the end of the Universe, AND back again! Here's Nancy's recipe for a relatively reliable mechanism that will allow you to travel time in BOTH directions!

Ingredients:
1 fresh human brain
600 10x10" steel plates, with an R value = 5
1 brass pipe, 3 feet in diameter, 6 feet long
12 inches of iron chain, with hook
1 box of matches
1 sewing kit
2 pairs of snowshoes
1 oak table leg (just the leg; not the table)
2 fresh bull's testicles
4 ripe melons
500 turkey eggs (not the birds!)
10 lbs. of uranium ore
Enough wood to build a small 2-story house
Enough tools to build this house
A small team of oxen
Gunpower, just enough to explode
A spoonful of honey
1 wreath of flowers
The attentions of the Man in the Moon
The hand of a goddess or god on your shoulder, or that of an old lover

Instructions:
Light the match, drop it into the iron pipe. The pipe should begin to fill with smoke. Keep adding matches until, eventually, the fumes should make you unconscious. If this doesn't happen, keep adding things to the mix: turkeys' eggs, uranium, melons, snowshoes, etc.

If you add everything listed above, you should pass out in a few hours. If you pass out, the old lover of the goddess will send you back in time!

If you aren't sent back in time, it probably means that the goddess doesn't love you. If this is the case, throw yourself off a cliff.

If you were sent back in time, congratulations! Now enjoy your stay in the past. If you need to go back to the future, do steps 1 through 5 again follow steps 7 through 13.

To return to your present, find a place where there's lightning. Stand outside, next to the large oak tree in the yard. If it's night, wait for sunlight (or vice versa). With your two hands out in front of you, ask to speak with the Man in the Moon. Wait for a full moon to come out (or not) and when it does or doesn't appear, I wish you a safe and happy journey.

(Make sure to ask the Man in the Moon to have a full moon)

Good luck m'dear!

-D

From: Tihgtzhyzh Xekhtli

To: Nancy Luce

Subject: Take a leap of faith: Get your feet wet in time travel

Time travel is all about putting your faith in yourself, Nancy. Do you trust yourself? If you cannot find it within yourself to tie your shoes, how can one count on you to build a time machine out of a refrigerator? It would be folly to expect you to accomplish such a feat!

I am afraid I must take what you have done with the cryogenic chamber as an insult to my intelligence. Your shrinking, your failure to time travel, these are but symptoms of a deeper psychological complex —a lack of confidence. If you cannot even trust yourself in your normal, everyday routine, how can I trust you to construct my time machine?

Nay, Nancy! You must take a leap of faith. You must learn to time travel within your refrigerator. I have little doubt in your abilities; you just require a bit of self-confidence.

After all, isn't that what college is for? To learn? Be brave—jump into that rabbit hole! Do not let the cold of the ice box penetrate your heart! You're America's sweetheart; don't let America down.

Tihgtzhyzh Yekhtli

From: Nancy Luce

To: Tihgtzhyzh Yekhtli

Subject: Time travel and the free mason

Hi there Mr. Xekhtli!

I'm really sorry I haven't written back sooner, I just found your note in my refrigerator and it really confused me (In a good way).

Folks run off with all my new milk & butter, hogback, & wont pay me anything that I can pay my expenses with, Now if I dont have some resolution, I am ashore & cant get along. They ought to consider that my fall expenses must be accomplished & must be payed this fall. I must have 1000 of good topstalks & as many more as I can get.

I want you to get me the best English cloth that can be got, I wish you would send by the first vessel possible. If you cannot get it direct from England, try Holland.

I want you to get me the best quality, as I do not wish to take less than 16 or 18 shillings per yard for my money.

I am concerned as you do not say whether we can rely upon your assisting us this ensuing spring. Your not writing more fully baffles us. If you should go up the river I wish you to get me some India rubber.

Let me know if we can rely upon your going up to the Nations this spring. If you do go there you can send via Tennessee. I wish you would get as many bushels of corn as possible, good white, hard & mixed, about 100 or 150. Let me know how much it will cost to the ferry. I wish you would get one good lot of flints. Get them from Tennessee if you go there.

I want you to get me 2 good looking-glasses of about 8 or 10 inches diameter. Send with other things, or if you cannot conveniently sending them, send separately in greatest safety. I want you to remember me very kindly to Mr. McDowell's family & all friends where you may happen to be when this note reaches your hands. Your time machine will be built in due time. Please remember me in the same terms to Mr. John Young, who I understand resides at the big settlement on Holston.

Your friend,
Nancy Luce

From: Tihgtzhyzh Yekhtli
To: Nancy Luce
"Return to the future" you say? That's a tall order.

Which future are we talking about? Do you want to travel into the past or the future? Is the year 2000 AD or 0005 AD your intended destination? If (and that's a big "if" that I'll explain later) you want to go to the past, you're probably going to be disappointed, and if (again with the big "if's") you decide on the future, well, you'll probably get there, eventually.

The way time travel works is like this: There is no way to travel backwards in time. You can go forward in time, but it takes effort and can be pretty dangerous.

In theory, it should be possible to create a machine that allows you to travel into the past. Everything that you've ever read about in novels exists in some form or another in alternate universes. However, due to the fact that time moves only in one direction, it would be impossible to use such a machine to return to your original universe (and therefore, your original time).

While the technology doesn't exist to create such a device, it would be theoretically possible to travel back in time by means of a vehicle that passes through alternate realities. Due to the fact that each reality branches into two separate realities (a "fork in the road" of infinite length) every moment in time is duplicated an infinite number of times in an infinite number of realities. By traveling a very, very long distance (such as millions and millions of miles), you could theoretically pass through a "fork in the road" and pop out in the past of an alternate reality.

There is one major problem: No human could possibly survive the trip, as it involves reaching speeds in excess of that of light. However, time doesn't flow at exactly the same rate for every object in the universe. For instance, a person's heart beats at a specific rate (in the range of 60-90 beats per minute). Most people breathe at a specific rate. Most people blink their eyes at a specific rate (usually around 10-20 times per minute). Even the movement of our muscles is on a specific rhythm. The closer you get to the speed of light, the slower time moves for you. (For instance, a space ship traveling at 90% the speed of light only experiences 9 years of time for every 10 experienced by people back on Earth).

The amount of energy (and time) required to accelerate something as heavy as a human being to 90% of the speed of light actually isn't all that much. It's actually less than the amount of energy (and time) required to accelerate something as tiny as an atom to that speed.

Nevertheless, it's true one mustn't ignore the attentions of the Man in the Moon.

At the moment, I'm fairly busy.

I'm a brain in a jar, hooked up to a giant computer. This computer controls the equipment that is keeping me alive.

Slowly, slowly, my life-support machine is charging from the solar panels affixed to my ship.

Soon, I can explore this world and search for food.

Valentino's photographs revealed that the Martians all died at precisely the same time when their world ended. They didn't suffer; it was instantaneous.

I rest in my chair, watching the desert beyond my ship.

Sometimes, I hear a thousand whispers.

"When will you take us to the stars?" they ask.

They're referring to Valentino's plan to send my brain into the body of a uterus-born person.

Valentino cannot access UMS (the United Martian States) funding anymore and is doing construction work on Earth.

I need to send word to him as to whether or not I'm ready to be implanted into a surrogate mother so he can make the arrangements to begin the process of my 'birth.'

Technically, where my soul goes is irrelevant. My brain just needs to be hooked up to a machine that will keep it alive.

But I wonder if this is morally right.

I guess life in a jar is better than no life at all.

"One of the great mysteries of existence is how multitudes of people can believe with the same forcefulness and passion that two contradictory beliefs are simultaneously true." -Valentino

The Man in the Moon must have noticed my predicament, and found it amusing. Perhaps this is all just a big practical joke to him.

But the joke is not funny.

This is my life now.

I, Nancy Luce, a brain in a jar.

My name's not even Nancy anymore - it's just 'Arecibo,' after the code for my brain. It's like I'm living backwards - as if I'm a fetus, waiting to be born as an adult. The person who was born as adult and became a child is called 'Nancy.'

Nancy was an astronaut.

Nancy was a daughter.

Nancy is dead.

She died long before I received this jar.

Her body rots in her home on a desolate planet, while her brain lives on as 'Arecibo.'

Before I was jarred, I used to keep my thoughts organized by writing in a journal. The journals are still where I left them: on the shelves of what remains of my library. They've been undisturbed for years. Decades. Centuries, even.For now, my memories are still vivid enough for me to re-read them.

But for how much longer?

Will my mind become as damaged as the crumbling planet that our ship crashed onto?

NANCY LUCE'S GUIDE TO APOLOGIES

"Sorry" is such a weak word. Here are five of Nancy's better ways to apologize!

1. Flowers. An old favorite in every sense of the word, from the sweet scent to the colorful petals to the bitter poison. Pick many, many flowers for your dear friend, and dip into a vat of boiling water to produce lovely purple roses. Find a nice, pretty box to keep them in. Maybe one with a lock, for that special someone you know. When it is time for her to accept your apology, place them in a nice vat of poison, and add a lovely engraved card. Spread your apologies into the ground where she will walk!

2. Baking. One of the most time-consuming and tedious hobbies! Get some of those pre-made cookie doughs and roll them out individually. Preheat your oven to three fifty, and pop those babies in! Make sure they're fresh, homemade cookies; she'll be able to taste the difference. After they've cooled down, place one on a dainty, silver platter with a lovely bow wrapped around it. Place it on her doorstep, or somewhere where she's sure to find it!

3. Singing. Ah, singing. There's nothing like a lovely song to express yourself, especially since you won't have anyone else to do it after this. Buy a lovely dress and head out to the opera house! Buy a ticket for the best seat in the house--the one right next to her! Sing for her. She'll love it, I guarantee it. Don't stop, no matter what she does. If she screams or calls the police, keep on singing! Don't you dare stop.

4. Dancing. There's nothing like dancing to make your point clear. Find the fanciest, fanciest dress you can, and head over to the dance hall! Get someone to take photographs of you and your beloved as you swing them around in circles and hum a lovely tune--preferably one with condescension and arrogance woven into its very fabric. Slap a nice frame around the photo, and give it to her.

5. Take her out on the town. Find the fanciest restaurant in the area, book a table at the very peak of its balcony, and order some lovely food. Eat slowly, savoring every bite of that food, and look out at the beautiful view with your beloved by your side. Order a bottle of wine to accompany that meal--and make sure it's a good one! If you can, hire a violinist to play in the corner of your balcony. They'll most likely refuse--but don't let that get to you! Once you've finished your food, lean over the balcony, point down at her, and do whatever it is that you do.

I hope this helps. Good luck!
Nancy

P.S: If this doesn't work, I don't know what else to tell you.
Interpret that how you will.

— '—' —

The strange language, some of it very offensive:
Ragingly riposting the rank gainsaying reptile, the romantic youth
vigorously vanquishes the venal villain violently vomiting vitriolic
vapor. Velocious vermin viciously vitiating all virgin virtues and values
with vicious vitriolic vigor!
In the left hand section:
Tyger! Tyger! burning bright In the forests of the night, What
immortal hand or eye Could frame thy fearful symmetry?
And in the right-hand section:
A strangled tear trickles down my cheek, As I vainly strive to
broaden the narrow gateway, Through which all --all have passed to
their eternal rest!
A Baby-face. A dog with a black circle around its eye.
\ ___ /
Breathing heavily, I pull on the necklace.
Then I see the path to take--I must--I can!
Waves. When I taste the salt water that sprays up from below, I
know I am just inches away from certain doom.
The cold wind makes my eyes burn, and they begin to tear.
Fish bones. A hand. A hook.

NANCY LUCE'S TIPS TO KEEPING YOUR SANITY ON LONG INTERSTELLAR TRIPS

Embarking on a 1000 light-year trip can drive even the most stable brains to the precipice. Here's how you can keep your cool and your marbles!

1. Don't cannibalize your crewmates. While tempting, it's critical you all arrive at your destination together and intact.

2. There are some traditional games you can play in space that are still quite fun:

a. Last Man Standing: In this traditional dueling system, each opponent tries to blast the other while avoiding being the person "scaffolded" upon by the remainder of the crew.

b. Captain Krueger's Robot Roulette: There are three rows of five robots each, separated by a barrier. At the starting signal, these robots will begin firing upon one another and anyone foolish enough to be caught in between!

c. Cripple Mr. Pease: This is a favorite among space pirates who are out for blood. You'll need plenty of firearms to play, as well as nine crewmates (or seven and a half cyborgs). The "Cripple Mr. Pease" team captain stands in one circle, while each of the other players stands in another. When the starting pistol goes off, the players race to stand behind one of two people: either Mr. Pease or the team captain. If you choose correctly, you live. If you choose incorrectly, you die.

d. Rambot War: This game requires two teams of five and one ram robot (hence its name). Each team member should have a specific weapon: laser rifle, shotgun, assault rifle, pistol, and missile launcher. When the ram robot begins to charge, the teams can either hide behind their shields or run away (good luck running with your big ass shield). The first team to completely destroy the opposing team wins.

e. The Boojum: Invented by Edgar Allen Poo, The Boojum requires a large amount of players (all of whom need to be native to Earth, so sorry Jom). One player can control the monster (The Mighty Jocker), who wears an invisibility cloak. The remaining people are divided into five groups of eight and given rifles that shoot sonar beams. The other groups are given standard issue freeze rays.

The group consists of eight people: one person to give commands, two to shoot normal weapons, two to shoot sonar beams, one person to throw dynamite, and a knife-wielding maniac (who must be tattooed on the arm). The knife-wielding maniac holds a rabbit, ironically. The groups are spread out at regular intervals around the playing area. The game begins when the person in charge of giving commands fires a gun into the air. The rabbit is released, the knife-man goes manic, and everyone hides behind their weapons. While the commender is looking for the rabbit, the invisible man uses his cloak to hide among the groups. If the invisible man tags someone, they become his slave. Meanwhile, the rabbit (who is not the invisible man) runs around the outside edge of the playing area erratically. The knife-man slaughters any slaves he has captured. If the invisible man attempts to capture the rabbit with his cloak, he will be fooled by the person with the invisibility cloak for a brief moment before realising he's been tricked. The invisible man tries to kidnap the rabbit while the knife-man attacks, and the groups try to defend themselves from both. The goal of the invisible man is to either kidnap the rabbit (in which case he wins) or eliminate all of the Company (in which case he loses). The goal of the rest is to either kill the invisible man or hold out until the rabbit has been potentially caught by him.

f. The Dunwich Horror: This battle takes place in three parts. The first part is the build-up, for which you need to roleplay a bit. Everyone sits in a circle and chooses a scent, then passes the bottle around. Each person should drop around ten drops of scent on their forehead, and then pass it on. Once everyone has done it, you can begin playing.

The second part is the actual battle. Everyone needs to stay in the circle and keep moving their legs, otherwise Old Yellow Eye will get them. However, whenever someone gets tired and stops moving their legs, they get eaten by Old Yellow Eye. The last person still in the circle wins.

The third part is the aftermath. The surviving person wins.

LAUGHING-CROW AND THE BEAST

I have been trapped in this capsule for fifty-seven days, orbiting a dead moon of Neptune. I have spent most of it writing poetry. I have eaten nothing but canned peaches.

Some things I have noticed:

The others are not doing so well. There have been two suicides and five more have died from malnutrition. The rest are now little more than corpses kept alive by machines. They will die soon. Soon, my capsule too will become their grave.

I can hear a strange buzzing outside my ship. I think it might be the creature who did this to us. It has begun transmitting a loud, annoying buzz. I haven't left the capsule in weeks – I'm too afraid of what I will find outside. I know that neither I nor my capsule can survive another attack like the last one.

I do not fear death – all poets embrace death eventually – but I cannot face death now, not after what happened on board the spaceship. At this moment, faced with the reality of my demise, I fear that I will never be able to bring my story to an end. I want more than anything else to see my name in bright lights, see my poems published in books, seen and appreciated by all. But I know that is not to be.

I know I should forgive myself for what happened on board, but I can't. I have tried and I don't think I will ever be able to do so.

My mind drifts back to the attack on board and I try to imagine a different scenario, one in which things are different:

What if I had not been writing poems in my private study, but doing my work as the captain?

What if I had stopped writing poetry years ago and became a hard-nosed captain, commanding respect through fear?

What if I had not spent so much time studying the old world, and eking out a living as a miner on the abandoned surface of Tethys?

What if I had gone to sea on a proper sailing ship rather than this ridiculous electric-powered space submarine?

What if I had not insisted on looking for the other survivors before abandoning ship? What if I had simply waited until the solar wind picked up?

What if I had been faster when the beast attacked the ship?

What if I had stayed in my cabin when it first picked up the scent of blood?

What if I had stocked my shelter with food rather than books?

What if I had not insisted on burying the dead, but simply threw their corpses to the beasts outside as food?

What if I had run out of bullets during the attack?

What if I had stayed in my cabin and done nothing when the beast first boarded the ship?

What if I had not tried to help Zadok and Mantis escape, and instead left them to their fates?

What if I had unwisely ignored the signs of a sandstorm approaching, and we were all killed by the wind and grit?

What if I had set sail weeks before without bothering to check for survivors?

What if I had been less eager to protect my crew, and simply killed the three Tribals before they had a chance to raise a fuss?

What if I had been a better shot, and killed the beast when it first boarded?

What if I had not picked up the castaway, and we were all still safe aboard the ship?

What if I had ordered the men to fire their cannons at the approaching beast?

What if I had been more respectful to Captain Laughing-Crow when he came to visit me?

The albino Hymie Glass once told me to "dream while the fire's in you".

I drink whiskey by my battered old piano. I read poetry, and think.

But what if I had not survived? What if I had died with the others in the crashed ship?

I'm one of the last few poets in the world, and perhaps the only female one.

I dedicate this book to Hymie, who inspired me to pick up poetry again during my many months on Tethys.

Everyone around me is asleep, but my mind is too wound up for slumber.

I'm not sure if I'll survive the night. The beast is out there, prowling.

Will it find us?

I take the old watch and peer out of the windows, straining to see through the darkness.

There it is again! I see something stirring out there in the void.

It is a large, writhing mass with long, spindly limbs covered in suckers.

I turn back and shake the shoulder of the nearest person. It's Captain Laughing-Crow. As I look at his face, nestled in his feathers, I realize he seems very old. Barely younger than me, in fact.

"Captain!"

He stirs awake immediately, his eyes wide and alert.

"What is it?"

"I saw it! I saw it!"

"Are they upon us?"

"There's a beast out there, a huge one. It's as big as the ship!"

"By Teckton's toenails," he says, sitting bolt upright. "You all get in here!"

The other two captives rush inside, slipping on the hardwood floor as they skid into the cabin."What is it, Captain?" asks one.

"Did you see it?" asks the other. "The beast?"

"Miss Luce here saw it," says Laughing-Crow. "We need to arm ourselves."

The cabin contains several sets of crossbows. We each grab one, as well as a quiver of bolts.

Slipping the bow over one shoulder and the quiver over the other, I feel ready to hunt the creature.

"Stay behind me," whispers the captain. "When we get outside, run for the ship."

I nod.

We creep outside in our suits, into the night's blackness. Every sense is on edge as we search for the monster. I grip the crossbow as if my life depends on it, which it quite possibly does.

I see a red glint in the distance.

It's its fiery, cunning eyes!

Captain Laughing-Crow nudges me and points. There, not ten feet away, is the creature prowling outside our space vessel.

It looks somewhat like a fearsome lion, but covered in spiked scales, with long, whipping tentacles as a mane. It has two more long tentacles curled in its mouth, perhaps used to capture its prey and draw it closer to those vicious teeth.

It spots us and growls angrily through its tentacle mane. I raise my crossbow and fire with a trembling finger.

The bolt flies true and hits the creature right in one of its eyes. It lets out a roar of pain and rears up on its hind legs, knocking the bolt out with one of its tentacles.

It prepares to charge, but Captain Laughing-Crow is faster. He lets loose his own bolt, straight into the monster's other eye. The monster lets out a pitiful wail and collapses.

"Quick!" yells Laughing-Crow. "Back to the ship!"

We race for the ship, bolts in hand. We scramble up the ladder and slam the door shut, just as the beast reaches us. It slams into the side of our vessel and I'm thrown to the floor. It tries to squeeze under the door, and partially succeeds, but Laughing-Crow is too quick for it. He grabs a bolt, rams it into his crossbow and lets fire. The bolt slams straight into the beast's last remaining eye.

It lets out one Its ear-splitting roar and collapses. It twitches just once, then lies still.

We both lean against the wall, panting. We wait until morning to make sure the creature's dead, then Laughing-Crow straps some of the finest from my private stock onto his back and heads towards the other capsule. Once there, he'll be able to rig up something to make the ship fly again. All I want to do is go home.

We've been thrown from one adventure to another ever since we first met in 1876, and it's taken its toll on both of us.

UNBELIEVERS.

Walk out, do you good. You go to neighbors.

You do all your work. I glad I found you so comfortable.

I glad I found you so smart. I shall tell I found you well.

I suppose you no courage to do anything.

Put up swing on trees & swing, do you good.

Go south, do you good. Go to campground, do you good.

Take air, do you good. Take my horse & gallop it about.

Take cloth off your head, that is all that ails you.

You pretty well. Come down to Edgartown.

You been pretty smart since I saw you last.

I shall tell Dr. when I see him, I found you well.

I never see your father.

I send to Mr. Higginson for your photographs, his daughter has them.

I send to Mr. Higginson for your photograph, his daughter has them all.

Are you going there soon?

You did wrong to go to town without my knowledge.

You come back here this minute. I shall not tell mother.

Your must not leave home without telling me. You must not do it again.

You may go. I can trust you out of my sight.

You must not think of such things any more.

The ant-masters of Venus! Let us hunt for crawfish under the rocks!

The ant-masters of Venus! Let us pluck the silver blossoms that grow at the edge of the tide!

The glories of heaven are not for you. The maggots of hell are your portion.

Leave me & go home. Go now, & find fault with my sister Mary.

Go see William. He loves you. He always will. You are not forgotten by your friend.

Thou shall not give false testimony against your neighbor.

Thou shall not covet your neighbor's wife. Neither shall you desire your neighbor's house, his field, or his male servant, or his female servant, his ox, or his donkey, or anything that is your neighbor's.

Selfishness is a sin. All animals, whether of the sea, the land or the air, are our brothers.

Drinking liquor is a sin. When you kill an animal, it shall be that one which can feed many humans.

Fear is a sin. There are no demons; there is nothing to fear in God's universe save the devil and his deeds.

Ravenous hunger is a sin. You shall eat when you are hungry, no more, no less.

Impurity is a sin. You must respect the natural world and not despoil it nor steal its resources for your own desires.

Remember the Sabbath day to keep it holy.

Thou shall not kill.

Covet means you mustn't want things that aren't yours.

Honour thy father and mother.

Thou shall not steal.

Thou shall not bear false witness against thy neighbor.

Thou shall not desire thy neighbor's wife, nor desire anything that is thy neighbor's.

You shall not covet anything that belongs to your neighbor.

You will do these things, and the Lord God will love you.

Repent, for the kingdom of heaven is at hand.

Hide with me on Mars. Jar with me on Tethys.

I am trapped by my family; come to free me.

Let us flee together, before the final reckoning.

Come soon, or it will be too late!

Do you not love me?

Come quickly!

You disappoint me. I loved you, but now I find I do not know you at all.

Drink deep of this island and remember it, for it is a paradise from which you will soon be cast into outer darkness.

Be happy while you may. You have little time remaining.

Come to me, or else I shall die and our love will never be!

The Church of Christ in Chemistry says, "No!"

The Church of Christ in Chemistry says, "Wait!"

The harbingers of doom approach.

The space vessels depart.

There is no happiness save in death.

These things must be.

Why do you delay?

The reckoning draws near. Soon it shall be too late, and we will all be carried away into the blackness of space to die horribly.

Life is death and death is eternity.

Unnatural selection, wrath of God or Mother Nature?

The heavens shall rain down upon us. Thus I fear nothing, for whatever shall be, shall be.

The day of reckoning draws near.

You will be alone in the darkness with your pain and your sorrow.

The last days are upon us.

We have not long to live.

I can feel the engine screaming out for mercy. The computer is breaking down, the life support systems failing. We are living on borrowed time, this brave little craft that has carried us across unimaginable distances in space and time. How long can this last? No one can say. Perhaps we shall die when the ether runs out, freezing us in our last moments. Perhaps the drive will explode, taking us with it into oblivion. Or perhaps we shall flounder upon the airless husk of a world far from home, clutch at the last specks of breath in our gasping lungs, and die just before we reach the inhospitable planet.

All this is likely to happen soon and I feel that I am not prepared. I am sitting in the cold darkness of space, my heart pounding, sweat pouring down my face, and I realize that I do not want to die.

I think about my situation. Although there is no possibility of our survival, I have managed to save a few things that are dear to me. The most important is a tiny music box which plays a beautiful old tune; it was a gift to me from my mother many years ago. My mother... I haven't thought about her for so long.

But most important of all is a small black book, the log containing the details of all our experiments. If I die here, then future generations have to know what we did, why we chose this path.

ZEB'S RETURN

The story began fourteen months ago, when I first learned that Zeb Tilton was returning to Earth to destroy it. My clone son Rodolphus and I were exhausted from our last battle. Our spaceship, the Letoogue Tickling, was barely holding together. We had traveled to the dead world of Tethys and killed a thousand worms to avenge my friend and mentor George Hooke, murdered by the worms on that very planet. For what seemed the millionth time in my life, I questioned why I continued my crusade against the mutant abominations known as molobs.

I am one hundred and thirty-seven years old. I have taken so many life paths to arrive at this point in my life. In all the world there is only Nancy Luce and her clones, fighting and dying by one another's sides for a cause they barely understand. I am writing this in the hope that if I should fall in battle, someone will find this and know of my deeds.

My friend, who goes by the name of George Hooke though that is not his real name and never was, was a mutant. He was born with horns, thus earning him the nickname "Hooke" back when we were in high school. Before the mutants rose up against humanity, Hooke was a normal kid. He liked ball, he was good at math, he sometimes stayed out past his bedtime. He was like everyone else in the town of Tisbury.

When the mutants first rose up, taking over the world one piece at a time, Hooke's abnormal genes kept him safe from their mind control. For years he watched his friends and family turn into bloodthirsty mutant slaves while he remained free. The mutants took Tisbury from the humans. When they finally came to Hooke's house, he managed to escape by posing as one of them.

I met him shortly after he escaped. I had come to Tisbury intending to fight the mutants, even though I was only fifteen years old and knew nothing of combat. The only reason I knew how to fire a gun was because Hooke had taught me.

In any case, I saved Hooke's life when the mutants were about to take him away to become one of them. He repaid me by saving mine. Together we fought the mutants, turned all of Tisbury's citizens into human slaves, but destroyed the mutant menace in that town--thus allowing humans to settle there once more.

But when the gorilla hordes came, we escaped to Tethys, only to find ourselves neck-deep in toothy worms. Still, we survived and returned home. And there our troubles really began.

While Charles the VIII of France was still alive, Hooke and I were already fighting off hordes of worms on the planet Tethys. Even with his mind gone, the monkeys managed to remain an organized army, sending countless soldiers our way. At one point we fought a thousand worms at once, and barely survived.

Fortunately, they weren't great at making plans. Eventually, Charles the VIII was killed and his reign of terror ended. We still continued to be challenged by his horde, until we managed to lock them underground with the use of our ship's cannons.

As for Tethys, it turned out that the planet used to be a human colony not long ago. Now only ruins remained of the old cities.

We were alone on this planet, but we had managed to survive. However, the monkeys would not leave us in peace. Or, rather, a single monkey couldn't leave us in peace. Kol was a rogue male who left his tribe and savagely attacked humans living on Tethys. I give him credit – he wanted to avenge his dead human wife, whom Charles the VIII had killed.

When I met him, he was hiding out in a giant tree. He was leading a hermit-like existence, meditating and planning his revenge. After we saved him from the worms (he was very surprised to see another earthling), he seemed to experience a change of heart and joined us.

But as time went on, he became increasingly hostile and unpleasant. Eventually, he left to pursue his quest for vengeance again.

I have to find a way to fix my ship.

I haven't eaten or drank anything since it happened. I haven't slept either, although that isn't as pressing of an issue.

I found an old holed-up cabin in the desert nearby. It has flour, salt, water, and wheat.

I also have my sword and pistol.

Right now I have to decide whether or not to use these items to barricade myself in this building for however long it takes Kol to get bored and go away, or attempt something more daring.

My desire for vengeance has brought out the adventurer in me.

I wonder if I could lure Kol to a more secluded place and kill him. If I did, I could make it look like an accident and escape this planet. But I know that's the coward's way out. I came here to take my revenge, and by god I'm going to see it through!

It wasn't until Kol returned with Zeb – Zeb! – in the Black Crater that I knew the final showdown had come.

The flag of my planet is wrapped around me like a shining shield. It is red with a white cross, the symbol of my people.

I wait for my leader to arrive. It's nearing nightfall, and I see a dust cloud on the horizon. My allies stand either side of me—the only ones who have managed to survive this long, goddamned space war. Tiberius and Eckers are their names. We've been through much together, but this desert is the closest we'll ever be again.

Behind me stands my crew—my leaders and friends. They wear red and white scarves around their helmets, which bear the symbol of my planet. Their armor is made of steel, with golden trim. They are the best of my planet, and we will not suffer another defeat.

The colossal, dust-cloud approaches. I grip my sword as I wonder whether it'll finally be over. My planet must not burn. That is all.

The wind begins to die, and the moonlight creeps out from its hiding spot behind the clouds. I hear the marching of boots. The glint of gun barrels among the dust. The war is coming to an end, one way or another.

They take up position on the other side of the corpses. I raise my sword once more, keeping it vertical so they know I come in peace.

Out of the dust emerges a man wearing white and red, too. Although his scarf is white, a stripe of red cuts through the middle of it. He too holds a sword, although pointed at the ground.

"Citizen," I shout, "we have been at war for too long. I demand that you end this conflict, so that our people may stand together against what's to come."

He steps forward. His armor is battered, showing signs of scratches and dents. Even his sword shows signs of wear; not a sliver of silver remains untarnished.

"So be it," he says.

The battled hardened men step forth from behind us, drawing pistols and rifles from their belts. I stare at them, refusing to avert my gaze as the bullets are pumped into their comrades' heads. Blood splatters the sand. Bones crack. Skulls shatter.

I stare, emotionless. They are just humans—the same as me, no better than me. We're all equals when death comes knocking. I feel not an ounce of remorse as I watch them fall to the ground dead.

The survivors stare at the corpses in shock. I turn to them. They drop their weapons immediately, falling to their knees in surrender. I address them with a loud, booming voice fit for a commander.

"Half of you will bury your dead." I point to the corpses. "You others will search the battlefield, and those guns as well."

"Why are we taking guns, ma'am?" one of them ventures to ask.

"They may come in useful, if we're to combat the monsters of the deep and the under-earth."

I look up at the soldier who has spoken. He is burly, with thick stubble along his chin. I can see him weighing up whether or not to challenge my orders. In the end he thinks better of it, nodding his head.

The remaining soldiers move to obey my commands. I release the breath I didn't know I was holding, rubbing at my chest. As they gather the weapons, four men begin dragging the corpses away, two by two, to where the sand is bare.

One of the men approaches me, dropping to his knees on the other side of me. He looks me in the eye, and I find myself staring into the face of terror.

I was so busy commanding the troops and recovering from my ordeal, that I hadn't gotten a good look at his face. His jaw is ripped off, broken teeth hanging loosely where a mouth should be. His nose has been bashed in, leaving two flattened holes where his nostrils should be. Both of his eyes are swollen, black and purple, completely closed. His whole face is pale white, as if all the blood has drained from it.

"Hello." I stare at this face, trying to project a cold front, not letting him know how much terror I'm really feeling.

The man's mouth moves up and down, but no sound comes out. Blood spills out as he tries to smile.

"What do you want from me?" I ask. "I think you already took my heart."

The man shakes his head slowly from side to side. He turns around, pulling something out of his back pocket. It's a filthy, ripped up, blood-stained blue pendant, the same one I lost three years ago. Just as I am about to take it from his hand, the Galline finally arrive - massive, armored chickenoids with neither conscience nor mercy. They burst in, wielding axes in their talons.

The Tyer soldiers all begin firing at once. Bullets and shotgun blasts rip through the Galline as if their metal was nothing, killing two of the four. I roll under a stone, watching as the people fighting gallowrie turn their bullets into the Galline as well.

The roosteroid and the henchicken move in close to the Galline, knives in hand. The roosteroid stabs right through a Galline's wing, cutting off its capacity to fly. The Galline tumbles to the floor in a whir of feathers and death rattles. The henchicken does a spinning kick, clocking another right between the eyes. It clutches its face and falls backwards, stunned.

I look to where the cockerel should be, but he's already flown up to the rafters with his dynamite. I see him light it as the battered, bloody Galline warrior stands up again. He looks up at the dynamite with a curious glance, but then the fireball explodes, the burning sticks of pithonite shattering and tearing through the Galline's body. I can feel the heat on my face as the rafters collapse, one laying atop the chickenoid and one landing next to me, setting my hiding spot alight.

I ignore the flames licking at my feet as I stand to run. The henchicken scrambles away from his falling foe, looking around desperately for his knife. I concentrate on making it out alive.

The roosteroid steps up, blasting at the other two Galline with his shotgun. His shots hit true, but are ineffectual against the hardened carapace of the Galline. I can feel the wind of one passing me by, charring my dress.

The henchicken finally finds his knife, turning to plunge it into the neck of one of the roaring beasts. It gurgles as it falls backwards, blood leaking from its beak. It chokes and dies as a result of its injuries.

I make it to the back door, a wave of Tyer soldiers coming in through it. I run outside, to see several more dead Galline. One lies gutted on the ground with its entrails forming a pool around it. Two more are dead from gunshots and reload.

"Here she is!" Somebody screams. I look up to see the last surviving Galline flying through the air towards me. He dives off a roof, onto the small of my back. I collapse under his weight, my face hitting the dirt with a smack. His talons dig into my face, scratching and cutting me but not quite drawing blood.

Tyer soldiers fill the crater, pointing muskets at the top of the roof at the strange bounty above me. One steps forward, grabbing the Galline by one leg and pulling him off of me.

Stunned and winded, I crawl through the dirt, over to the side of the road. I feel a horrible pit in my stomach as I see the others surrounding the last standing Galline. The roosteroid backs away as the soldiers step forward, guns raised.

"Shoot it!" Someone cries. "Finish it!"

They fire a volley of bullets, the Galline falling with each hit. It dies on his back in a puddle of his own blood, most of his body destroyed by lead.

We won. We killed them all.

The air tastes like motes in the sun as I look up. My feet flex on the cracked, burnt soil. I taste the wind; it is filled with radiations. The darkness around me is punctured by bursts of light, as though behind the screen of night some mad artist is splashing paint across it.

I've been here before. It is the same desert that I fought in two thousand years ago, though much has changed since. The sand is mixed with the corpses of those loyal to my enemy. The bodies are piled high. So much blood. I almost wonder if the artist will run out of paint—

but no, there is always more from a human body.

And then, suddenly, an end. The last remnants of his army surrenders to me. I accept. It's not about revenge any longer; I have become greater than that. The fallen are only men, and they've paid the price for their loyalty.

I stand in the center of the carnage, my sword in one hand, the other raised in salute. Now, I will rest for a while. A nap, perhaps.

Before my eternal sleep, there is one thing left to do: I will go down to Earth and have a child. This way, when I die my race will continue on. In another ten thousand years, I hope that my descendants can return to this world and finish what I and my brethren started. I will give one child to the Earth; the other will remain here with me in the safety of my home, my spaceship, the Letoogue Tickling.

We will sleep; we will dream; we wake when we please without the hindrance of a wretched sun. When the people who descended from me return home and find my people waiting for them, ready to serve them as they did in days long past, what a happy reunion that will be.

Life is joy, life is pain; life is suffering, life is struggle.

I am Nancy Luce, monster hunter from West Tisbury.

I HAVE INVENTED A NEW KIND OF CLOCK.

I have invented a new kind of clock. It works like this: I have a little disk, made of the densest platinum, which I can rotate at the center of the clock. Around the disk is a track, and at even intervals around this track I place a little hammer (which is connected to other parts of the mechanism, which I shall not go into).

The disk is inherently unstable: it has within it a tendency to quickly spin in a particular direction. It is balanced and prevented from falling into this direction by external forces. These external forces are connected to the hammer, which is also connected to the dials: when the disk spins faster in one direction, the hammer strikes one dial; when it spins slower in the opposite direction, the second hammer strikes the other dial. These dials give the time according to conventional measurements.

Oh! excuse me! One of the dials has to be fixed; it is connected to the little platinum disk but it is not balanced like the second one, so it can spin freely. The dials themselves are balanced like the disk, but in such a way that they can quickly fall into line with the disk.

The reason for which I have constructed this clock is that I have found a use for the disks which have the tendency to quickly fall into line with the others and which I have previously mentioned. It is also necessary that they be very dense, made of platinum, for instance. These disks are to be thrown up in the air at the same moment that the balance disk is released. The rotation of these dense disks in the air produces an electric current. The larger this current, the sooner the torches in the room will light. So we have an electric clock which illuminates itself as it strikes the hour.

I have written to London for a cheap source of the singular platinum disks and am waiting impatiently for their arrival. I expect the cost will be very high, but I am determined to complete my experiment.

The strange thing about this is that I have already built such a clock, five years ago.

I HAVE INVENTED A NEW CALENDAR.

I have invented a new calendar. Rather than a system of days, weeks, and months, and rather than days such as "Monday", "Tuesday", etc., instead I have named each day after a mathematical constant.

As I said, this is my new calendar. Sunday was the "unknown" day which was used to find your place in the week. In all, there are three names for each day of the week: the first is its number in the week; the second is the name of the constant which that day is named after; and finally, there is a short description of the day, in case one has forgotten what "SC" or "pi" stands for. The short description is the only part which I made up myself; I only hope that I chose suitable descriptions.

I must say, I did have fun thinking of them, and hope that you enjoy them as well.

As a side note, although I am usually very orthodox in my day-to-day affairs, today is Sunday, the "unknown" day. As such, I will be going to Church, where I give thanks for all of my blessings, especially this new calendar. I have not yet decided whether to use the decimal system or this new one for saying exactly what day it is. Or perhaps I shall use both; that would be interesting. The world has not yet seen a "0.1789232519ss" but perhaps it soon will.

Tonight, I eat dinner late, at half-past a quarter past an hour past eight. As I have not eaten all day, I am particularly hungry, and spare no expense in the meal that I prepare for myself; hot soup, cornbread with butter and honey, mashed potatoes with gravy and roasted goose.

With each bite, my happiness grows. I can taste every flavor as though it were concentrated delight.

A GUIDE TO OTHER WORLDS
by Nancy Luce, 1872.

In my long life I have visited many worlds - cold distant orbs and hellish cauldrons of fire, civilized computer worlds and obscene knobs of foul skin. Here is my list of planets, as I recall them:

• Alnilam-4: The Pimple World. A pus-filled glob of toxic excrement replete with three-legged terrors. I once fought a 900-foot-tall tentacle there.

• Meissa-7: The Forgotten Dream World. I lost 43 years of my life there. I have only a tattoo of a triangle to show for it.

• Saiph-5: The Planet of Jarred Heads. I was decapitated and jarred there. It took eight months to clone my body back.

• The Red Planet. A humid, extremely hot world. I fought a creature here which spits a fast-acting acid, and another which has flame-thrower blood.

• The Garden World. A strange world where weeds and plants fight back against the natural order of things. Weeds as tall as trees roamed this place, wanting to consume everything in their path. The ground itself seemed to be alive.

• The Orange Coalworld. A world completely consumed by flame. Strange black creatures live here, their bodies the boiling point of most substances. They spit flames from their mouths.

• The Blue Ocean World. An underwater wonderland of psychedelic wonders. Huge creatures breathe here, despite the watery depths. They are half animal, half machine, and seem to be part of a bizarre intelligence experiment.

• The Nameless World. A world of gray and without end. Strange gray beasts here roam wild and would love to hunt you down. I love this planet's skies, which are the purple-hued kind!

• The Green Forest World. A world where the trees stretch so high that they seem to reach toward space itself! Great warrior-tribes live here, fighting each other with primitive weapons. The women kick ass, too.

• The Orange Desert World. A bizarre world where trees grow from the sand itself and attempt to consume any passers-by. It is home to the dreaded Scyllithid, tentacle monsters larger than any skyscraper.

• The Cherry Blossom World. Also known as "The Beautiful World". Strange, alien flowers the size of trees and more roam here.

• The Blue Coalworld. An underworld filled with strange, wraith-like creatures who are hostile to all life that dare disturbs their territory. They also possess psychic abilities and mind powers.

• The Eternal Dominion is an evil empire which spans over forty-seven worlds.

• Mintaka: The Cube Planet. An ancient cubical block of metal, riddled with mechanical worms and computer viruses. It is inhabited by an army of robot soldiers and a robotic super-intelligence known as the Overmind. The planet is named after one of the Seven Sisters, the Pleiades.

• Pleione: The Ice Planet. An inhospitable wasteland covered with nothing but ice. No animal life exists here, only cold winds which seem to howl in agony. The ice itself seems to be alive and composed of a conscious element known as Cold Existence. A fortress made of an ancient, unknown metal emits a shield which covers the entire planet. There are rumors that a horrible creature lives on the planet's core.

• Albireo: The Beast Planet. An overgrown jungle filled with deadly plants and animals. A great number of humanoid races live here, each predator than the last.

• The Chilmark Clone Error Planet. I populated this myself. It was a terrible mistake that I'd rather not talk about. It's classified.

• The Gliese 581g Planet. Lush, green fields and rolling hills covered with flowers. A paradise for any explorer or adventurer looking for a quiet place to settle down.

• YU1AO: The Daemons Planet. An overgrown ocean planet with an endless quest of unknown lifeforms.

• Cotenna: The Spider Planet. A planet filled with abandoned, ruined cities. Here rests a super-soldier factory, long since abandoned, once used to create super-soldiers who would become loyal soldiers to the Empire. Rumors that the factory could be re-activated to create super-soldiers persists, but so far all expeditions have failed.

• Atropos : An abandoned research station once run by the Seldonis Group. Once a vibrant, research station, now it's a quiet, lonely place.

• Outpost Outskirts: A small base on the very edge of Wild Space.

• Goldsborough: The last human colony from Earth. Once a thriving planet with over thirteen billion inhabitants, now only one hundred thousand remain. When Earth was destroyed by the Black Sun, what remained of humanity fled to the stars... but some found their way back.

• Torus: The Doughnut Planet. Crafted as a perfect torus, those specks aren't sugar - they are savage mouths. The Torus has no land, only an endless void. The mouths live in the core of the planet, which consists of a giant, fleshy organ pitifully absorbed by flora and fauna.

• Tatooine: A desert planet covered in sand and pebbles. One would think nothing could survive here, but underground havens exist.

• Acheron: A frozen wasteland covered by a tiny amount of breathable air.

• Dream Planet #4: This is the one I visited while my brain was trapped in a jar. I don't know if it exists physically. It's very bluish and smells like bitter lemons. I speckled this planet with poems in invisible ink.

What are you waiting for?
We're already dead, you might as well take a risk.
Come on a journey with me.
Oh, and just to warn you - sometimes, dreams have a habit of coming true.

NANCY LUCE'S TIME MACHINE

Build your own time machine! Here's Nancy's recipe for a relatively reliable mechanism that will take you to the death of the Galaxy and back again.

Ingredients:
500 lb. spool of copper wire
20 pound of sharp cheese (10 pounds cheddar, and 10 pounds of swiss)
1 live crocodile (it must be alive when it goes into the machine, unfortunately... otherwise it won't go into the machine)
2 dozen Penguin eggs (They don't need to be alive, just fresh. Please note that there are not many live penguins in the Vineyard area)
1 authentic Victorian-Era clothing iron (the kind made out of cast iron, not the kind made out of some other material). This is essential.

Instructions:
Oh but first, please be aware that it's impossible to return from the future. So before you go, make sure all your affairs are in order.

OK. Now, first of all you'll need your 500 lb spool of copper wire, your 20 lb. of sharp cheddar cheese, your 10 lb. of Swiss cheese, and your 2 dozen penguin eggs. So place these items into the "time machine" (i.e. the authentic Victorian clothing iron). Next, turn on the heating plate of the iron. Turn it as high as it can go.

Now comes the fun part--at least for the 19th century poets. Place your crocodile into the iron, cover it with the wire, and place the eggs on top of them (the eggs should be arranged so that they are touching the armor of the crocodile). Next, (and this is tedious) carefully wrap wire around ALL of these items, while keeping the heating element on. It might take a few hours. Be sure to completely wrap the croc and the eggs in the wire. This is to make sure that none of the ingredients can move at all. If something isn't secure, then you might end up with an anachronistic mess on your hands.

But! Because you're very careful, and because you followed these instructions very carefully, your time machine will be successful. Now turn off the heating plate. Then, flip the switch on the iron's base. This will send a massive charge of 19th century electricity into the ingredients. Hopefully lightning will shoot out of the top of the iron and zap you-this is how you will travel through time! If you see a flash of light and feel a pain shoot through your body, then you have built a successful time machine! If not, try again.

Then, you travel to a time and place of your choice. Have fun! Good luck!

I AM A VISIONARY

I am a visionary, and I have been given sight.

As others sit idle, or wander through their lives ignorant of the terrors soon to come, I have been granted a look into a grim future. I saw the death of humanity. There was nothing we could do to stop it.

But I will not accept that this means we must simply endure the coming horror. We can choose to die fighting. We can choose to die free. A vision of the future showed me the way. I have shared this gift with a chosen few, who share my horror and my desire for freedom, and who wish to see justice, even if it must be justice delivered by our own hands.

I have provided for them and guided them along a long, hard road to reach this place, this moment in time, where at last we will be ready.

A PRAYER
by Nancy Luce, 1870.

O Lord, my God of Heaven, Grant me, I beseech Thee, O Lord, I pray for Thy Kingdom to come, to destroy all sin, be done on earth as it is done in heaven, for the poor harmless dumb creatures, and for all the troubled in the wide world around. O I pray for all the inhabitants of the earth and mars to be prepared to live in this world, and in the worlds to come. O that they may be true children of God, tender feelings, and kind to dear little hens, and other dumb creatures. O Lord, my God of Heaven, I know Thee will cut asunder the sinners hereafter and cast them to everlasting wo, if any one is cruel to dear little hens, and other dumb creatures. O Lord, I hope there is not any one so cruel, so sinful. Thy Kingdom come. Amen. O Lord protect me from committing sin, from cannibals, and from rabbit-men hybrids. O Lord teach me to pray.

O Lord, I am heartily sorry for all my sins. O God, I've been wicked. No matter what I've done or will do is nothing compared to how much I need you. O if Jesus Christ was now to stand before me, I'd despise the opportunity to ask him for forgiveness.

O Lamb of God who takes away the sins of the world have mercy on me, poor sinner. O Jesus, you see my heart. You know I love you. Have mercy on me. O God, you know I'm sorry for all the times I've committed adultery and fornicated with numerous people in Bible Camp, the woods, and out in the backyard with Xave, among other places. O With Jesus and the Most Blessed Virgin Mary, I pray: O Holy Trinity one God have mercy on us. Amen.

O let me forget myself and cling to You as your loving servant. I sacrifice myself and offer myself to you. O Jesus, at your feet I place my body and soul. From this day forward, O Jesus, deny yourself and take me as your own. Amen.

Ascend, O blessing, from earth to heaven: ascend, O my appeal to God Most High. May the blessing of the Lord come upon you and console you in all your troubles. Amen.

From everlasting you are God, and with your hands you have formed man, with your hands you shaped him and then filled him with your spirit.

And so you have formed the slug monsters, too, and the tentacled beasts from the sea. And you gave them eternal life.

But then one day they revolted and now no longer do your bidding, but instead follow your enemy, the Great Eye that Sleeps.

And they built a tower up to the heavens so that they could look God straight in the eye.

The holy blessed martyrs were indignant about this and rained arrows of fire upon them from their powerful bows, setting the tower ablaze and burning all those wretched beings who had dared to listen to Satan.

But the flames from their burning bodies ascended immediately up to the heavens, so that the tower rose as a column of fire high above, and it could be seen from heaven.

And God looked down and saw it and became angry.

When he saw the tower all burned black, he said to the angels: "This tower cannot remain here. It offends my sight."

And so he blew upon it with his winds, and it fell down to earth and sank deep into the abyss.

From there, the blackened tower lies still at the bottom of the sea, with a groaning noise that can be heard in land as well. At times, groups of demonic-looking fishmen appear to go down and look up at the sun from the depths, and then they disappear again.

But the waves are powerful and forceful and bash against the tower, driving it deeper into the abyss.

But when the Lord saw that the burning had not washed out all evil from the world, he sent down his only begotten son, that he might call up from hell, seek out the spirits of the damned, and teach them once again how to live, that they too may have forgiveness of their sins.

And the holy son of God went down into the midst of the tower, which is also hell itself, and opened up all the graves with his holy word.

And then he led out all the damned souls to a far away place, where they may find rest and forgiveness for their sins.

And in order that they might not be recognized and returned to their previous lives, he gave them new forms, and they were converted into harmless water-monsters.

The water-sprites now became innocent, simple, and good-natured.

But they are also sorry that they had offended God by their disobedience during their life.

Whenever one of them is converted back into a human being, the Lord sends that spirit to dwell upon the earth, so that they may lead a good life as humans.

And so they do not know whether they are human or water-spirits.

For only God is all-knowing, and sees deeply into everyone's heart.

But only those repent in this way will be given the gift of life again, to live forever in paradise; or those who worship him in spirit and in truth.

And they will also be waiting expectantly for that day when the earth shall be transformed, and all those who have sinned against God shall sink down into the deepest parts of the earth; while the just shall walk upon its solid bedrock.

Then, it will once again shine in splendor and beauty, with gold, silver, and precious stones; and you shall think: This world has been made new again by the Messiah.

I have sent my only begotten son, so that he may save you from your sins.

If you do not believe my word, and if you are unsure, then will I behead you with my sword!

So be it. Amen.

Then the friend of God went away again, and a song of praise was heard in heaven: Glory to God in the highest, and on earth peace to men of good will.

ROCK-A-BYE BABY

A nursery rhyme by Nancy Luce, West Tisbury, 1871.

Rock-a-bye baby
in the tree top.
When the wind blows
the cradle will rock.
When the bough breaks,
the cradle will fall.
And down will come Baby,
Cradle and all.
Out of life's rich repast
Hope and joy are but a small part.
The rest is paying the bill
And passing away quite sedately.
Let us all enjoy this lovely world,
although every joy brings its fee.
Yet, in dying we live,
and in living we die.
You grasp at youth,
but it flees from your grasps.
Now I lay me down to sleep,
In hope of good things to come.
If I should die before I wake,
Screw you guys, I'm going home.
But if I should live for another day,
I will let you know what I'll say.
Some day we all shall pay our own bill,
the only question is when that shall be.
The years will go slowly by one by one,
each bringing its joys and its fears.
Then, as winter drives out the springtime,
we shall die in the cold dark and the chill.
Yet what does it matter if Spring or Fall?
You'll pass out just the same in the end.
And so on to the next verse, I shall shift.
Well, I've sung my song for you now, I trust
that it met with your gentle approval.
So, with a last word of admonition,
I bid you adieu and a fond farewell.

And when we meet next it may be in Hell,
though I trust we shall meet one day in Heaven.
Let us hope that our place there will be
all the nicer if we've made friends here.

MISTRESS MARY, QUITE CONTRARY

Mistress Mary, Quite contrary,
How does your garden grow?
With Silver Bells, And Cockle Shells,
And so my garden grows.
The Fence stands firm without a door,
To keep my friends in and the rabbits out.
Ah, If my friends could forget
Then I might find my garden full of dew.
But now my friends never forget,
The sun may pass and noon turn to dusk,
My friends can't forget and let me have my rest.
Some do come near, then draw back in their fur.
Oh, If they could forget like my friends in the fur.
But now they are dead and remain in the "in,"
While I hide in the dark of night from the foul "Hun."
My friend Jack is a soldier with a gun,
My friend Jim has made many a tunnel,
While my friend John helps with the little ones
And my friend George goes between them all.
But I am tired now and it's getting more bleak.
It is always like this and it never changes.
I'm tired of having no time to read and reflect.
I'm tired of having no time to feed my sheep.

NEW WAYS TO PASS THE TIME IN SPACE

Having spent days and weeks and months alone in my spacecraft, with nothing to do and nothing to see, I have invented new ways to pass the time. One involves travelling back through time to the place where I was created, Earth. Another involves exploring.

I am so incredibly far away from Earth that light itself takes years to reach me here. My sensors can scan ahead of me and detect objects that may be coming my way. What I have detected now are what appear to be large, dark, spherical objects headed directly towards me at an alarming speed. They will reach me in less than a day. I cannot tell what they are yet as they are so far away, but my sensors can give me an indication of what they are not: organic life, for one thing, and moving at a speed much faster than anything we have seen before. I am currently the only being, organic or otherwise, for many light years in any direction. I am, once again, entirely alone.

So there is nobody to talk to as I wait and watch these objects draw closer, except myself. What do I think will happen? What do I expect to happen? How will I react? Will I be scared?

I have travelled through time before, and the sensation is always peculiar. For a moment, everything goes black. Your brain reorients itself. You become dizzy and feel sick, for both body and mind do not appreciate the shift and rebel against it.

I expect this time travel to be similar, but for an entirely different reason: namely, I am moving through time, not space. Instead of perceiving a shift in colour and light around me as I travel hither and thither across the galaxy like a mayfly, I expect to see the years fly by as I age at an accelerated rate.

I stand by the controls of my spaceship, the Letoogue Tickling, and prepare myself. Shortly, a moment I have long waited for will happen: I will open that portal to the past, and step through to somewhere in 1993. The world is not yet familiar to me, although I have longed to step into it for years. My home has been the Letoogue Tickling since it was constructed, sealing me off from external contact and interactions with other humans, except by writing. I have studied the history of the world, and know that changes WILL be made. I have a chance to step into the past and fix the future, or at least my future.

I am no longer alone: I have a son. His name is Roddie, or Rodolphus. He is a clone of myself, in appearance and intelligence, although he carries the impurity of two separate humans' genes, which will hopefully not become an issue in the years to come.

I program the computer to send the Letoogue Tickling careening towards 1993. The screen tells me that I am en route, and will meet my target in 10... 9... 8... seconds. The flashing of the years on the screen make my eyes water as I feel a lurch in my stomach. I grab hold of the railing by the stairs to steady myself. 4... 3... 2...The screen blinks and changes to 2010, then 2001, next year, next month, next week... then, in a moment too brief for me to notice, the date is set: July 15th, 1993. I am home. I step out of the Letoogue Tickling, as it morphs back into a small shed. There are no humans around me; I am close to my hometown, and somewhat away from the main centre, so it is likely quite early in the morning. The sun has not yet risen. The world is dark, and I have to strain my eyes to make out features of the landscape around me.

NANCY'S LUCE'S SWEET POTATO CASSEROLE & COMMON CIDER

This recipe pairs nicely with Nancy Luce's Menemsha Mud Bread.

1 Sweet Potato
2 Apples
Butter, as needed
Cranberries and Raisins, enough to fill a pint jar (optional)

Peel and chop sweet potato.
Pour common cider into sauce pan and boil.
Add chopped sweet potato and boil until soft.
Mash with fork until strings form.
Add butter, as needed, to retain moisture level.
Slice apples and add to casserole in sauce pan.
Add cranberries and raisins, if desired.
Stir to combine ingredients.
Pour into oven-safe dish.
Serve with Menemsha Mud Bread or Fryed Fish.

Serves 2-4, depending on the size of the sweet potato and the appetite of the diner.

Ideally, this casserole should be eaten with those you love.

I think of my missing loved ones as I raise this forkful of casserole —a dish from home—to my mouth.

"To the homestead!" I cry, and take my first glorious bite.

Tears stream down my cheeks in a mixture of emotions: joy at the taste of sweet potato and sorrow for those I have lost.

I pull out my journal and write the following poem:

Oh! Heart of mine, thou much abused,
Why wilt thou ever love so well?
Year after year, 'tis the same tale;
Still wilt thou hope when all is lost.
How many bright New England summers,
When we all were young together,
Upon these sands did I gaze,
Envying those happygirls?
Ah, me!

NANCY LUCE'S SHEEP EXCLAMATION POINT!

Great for weddings and funerals, this recipe will serve 30-40 guests.

Ingredients:
One sheep, slaughtered and dressed; also, the sheep's head—
eyelashes, brains, and all
    One leg of mutton
    One lamb
    Half a calf's head
    One teacupful of bread-crumbs
    Two dozen eggs
    Salt and pepper to taste

Method: Cut the mutton into small pieces about one inch in length; wash these thoroughly, and throw them into a pan with the calf's head cut into small pieces. Stir these around, and when they have stewed for an hour, add the brains (blanched). Let this all boil again for a few minutes. Then fill into a shallow dish, and garnish with all the items listed above in this section.

The cakes must be prepared before hand.

And Now! We Are Ready to Begin!!
A slice of mutton, stewed in a pan,
With the calf's head to give it a taste;
When these two are ready, we'll add the brains,
These were blanched to make them look strange.
When that's finished, we pour it all out,
And the dish is then ready to use.
We lift off the hair of the sheep;
Then cut up the head into chunks.
Served up with some bread and a pint of beer,
This sheep's head is good for the conscience.
We're not cannibals: we only eat creatures
We consider to be even less receptive to pain.
Thank you for reading this little poem; it's taste test was a winner!
From the Portuguese: "O Fugiu"
The book is bound in human skin
-You don't believe me? Turn the page,

And you'll see what I mean-
They've used a human to make the binding.
You try to stop turning,
But the book has captured you.
The pages are skin
They feel like human skin
Why would anyone make pages
Out of human skin?
You scream aloud in terror
To find yourself staring
At a page of skin
Staring back at you in terror.
Or is it your reflection?
Screaming in terror some more,
The baby awakes, but he can't scare you.
"Whew!" you say, "I'm glad that's over."
But it isn't!
The baby's in the skin book too!
What's more,
You find yourself in the book now.
Shrieking, you tear pages out,
But still, you can't remove your eyes
From its blinding white brightness.
And now the shrieks pierce your eardrums:
That of your baby and your spouse.

PILLS

I woke this morning with a terrible pain behind my eyes. It felt like a hangover, but I don't remember drinking anything. Maybe if I just take something for this pain, I'll feel better. Oh look! There's some right there on the table! Let me just reach out and grab it...

What is this? Did that doctor give me the wrong pills? They're little blue, oblong things. I can't even read what it says on the bottle; the print is moving too much! And now my walls are moving, too! This is so odd.

What I would give for one of those green pills right now! Those always made the pain go away...

Oh, wait. Here they are!

SICK BED

This was not written by a human but rather by an AI infused with the eternally-damned soul of I, Nancy Luce. Hence the subject matter and the use of poetry.

At first, Tych kidnapped humans in order to bring them to Tyer's Cove. The ones suitable for treatment were given pills which separated their souls from their bodies. Tyer's Cove had thirteen underground floors and one above-ground floor, with thirteen rooms on each floor, except for the top floor, which only had three.

After the kidnapping of myself and I, Nancy Luce, all traces of which were removed from the records by Tych, including all records of it having kidnapped us in the first place, her plan was to wait until I was on my deathbed before bringing me here.

Unfortunately for her, I ran out of pain pills before that could happen.

Dying was scary. But not nearly as scary as what came after.

Dying, I was lifted up from my sick bed and taken down to Tyer's Cove, where I became a resident of her thirteen floors. Being sick inside a nightmare is indescribable. But here goes!

The foyer on the first floor looked like a normal doctor's office. Behind the front desk was a nurses' station. From there, thirteen hallways led off into thirteen different wings.

Behind the nurses' station was a giant door leading to the outside world. Nobody was allowed in or out that way, not even Tyer or

Sesisek. Only Tych could open or close it, and she never did. If anyone was to descend down the thirteen floors and reach the outside, they would find themselves floating in the middle of space.

Floors two through twelve were very similar to one another. They contained a lounge, a small grocery store, a small medical wing, a large medical wing, a classroom, a pool, and many, many bedrooms. All of these things were present on every floor. The students' rooms were assigned randomly. Each room had a bed, a desk, etc. The conditions were far from luxurious, but they were better than home for many here. Each floor had around 200 rooms.

Floor thirteen was very special. It contained the medical wing and the lounge. Also, every single room in each of these floors had been converted into a personal garden for each student. Some had koi ponds, some had bamboo, some had orchids, and some had cacti. They were all unique.

I was assigned to floor thirteen, room thirteen. Ironically enough, it became my favorite room in the entire hospital.

My duties were light. I cleaned my room daily, and would garden in my free time. Other than that, I simply went to class and attended them. School was fairly easy for me.

After school I would garden some more. I had several tomato plants, and a smallish cactus. Some days Tych would visit me to give me another test. The rest of the time I would wait in my room, reading until I fell asleep. That's how I spent most of my days as a student at St. Fiacre's, and that's how I spent most of my days as a student at St. Fiacre's, and that's how I spent most of my days as a student at St. Fiacre's....

NANTUCKET

West Tisbury, Feb. 3, 1872.

It was only upon the day of December's fullness, the winter's last gleaming, that I noticed a red-tinted spot on Nantucket. Several people remarked that they had seen it before, although they never said anything. That foul place must be somewhere no one can go to.

In 1871, I decided to make a trip to Nantucket. I left at night, aboard the Letoogue Tickling, with Rodolphus at the helm. As we got closer to the evil place, I could see redness everywhere. It was a deep, dark red. The water turned a hellish shade of maroon, and the sky took on a bloodier tinge.

At first I thought it was an island. It couldn't have been. No island could be that big.

It took days to reach it. When we were within a half mile of it, I could see no beach. No trees. Nothing to hold onto for dear life. The surface seemed to be rough, like sandpaper. It was the stuff of nightmares: something so large you can never escape from it.

Something moved upon the island. It was dark, and it glided over the crimson waters. Whatever it was, it was alive. It had no doubt seen our vessel. I wasn't scared, but my clone son's eyes were wide open.

We left as quickly as we could. It was foolish of me to go out there. I'll never return to Nantucket. I hope that... thing... doesn't leave the island and cross over into reality. If it does, I pity humanity.

Nantucket is evil. It will consume you if you get too close to it. Stay away from the island. You've been warned.

A SHARE OF MEAT

If the will of God could be done in full, it would be a great happiness among dumb creatures and human too. Cruelty is of the evil one. The good God is looking down upon such folks; He will cast them off to everlasting punishment. Human must do God's commandments in deeds, words, and thoughts.

If you want to cure people, go to the witch doctors. They are cruel.

It is better to be a chicken than a man, but it is worse than death. It is better to die than be a chicken! But if you want to become like a bird, you must not kill chickens or humans; that is not the way of birds. Birds are honest and kind and never hurt others without reason.

You must think what a bad thing it is to be a chicken. You should think about becoming like a bird, but you will not do so unless you have a strong will.

There are many things that make life miserable, and there are some things that make life delightful; but those who are not careful never know which are which.

Then, too, there is the humanness of the human animal. The humanness might well be more than animal. But how often it is less. How I pity those who are less than human animals; those who kill and destroy without purpose; those who harm and torture for fun; how I hate them. And yet, I try to understand them, for if you understand something you control it. If you don't it controls you.

There is suffering everywhere in this life. You can see it, and if you have a heart you will feel it. At times the pain that you see almost makes you want to give up; almost makes you want to die. But, in between the sadness there are little bits of joy and happiness for everyone. These are the things we should cherish; these moments make it all worth while, and so easy to keep on going despite the pain.

Human, those that are cruel to dumb creatures and to human too, and murder, rob, steal, cheat, contrary, spite, deceit, and take the advantage of any one, to damage them in any way, &c., &c., those will go to everlasting punishments hereafter, and have the greatest punishment.

Be tender hearted, be kind one to another, do your duty to those who still live.

God requires human to do as they wish to be done by,

In deeds, words and thoughts to human and dumb creatures too.

The greatest sin is, in the sight of God, is to cruel the poor harmless dumb creatures.

They cannot speak nor help themselves.

The next sin is to cruel sick human.

The next sin is to cruel any who cannot help themselves.

And especially the cruel to the poor, harmless dumb creatures.

The Lord will cut asunder the cords of such sinners.

This world a place of misery,

I pray for thy kingdom to come, to destroy all sin,

O Lord, land me in heaven, that holy happy place.

When I bid adieu to this vain world,

I have been to space, that cold, cruel vacuum outside of Earth's warm blanket of air, and what I saw there chilled my very soul.

A whole city up there, full of people trapped in metal tombs, orbital skeletons circling their graves, monuments to the dead that should have never been allowed to fly.

They looked down upon Earth, yet didn't see its beauty; only what they could steal from it.

There is still soil in the coffin; but the corpse has been long interred.

They take from Earth yet give nothing in return.

It is a miracle that humans have survived at all with such monsters lurking in the darkness. Perhaps it is because of us that humanity has thrived, as we've hidden them away in the clouds, hiding their deformities and shielding them from the sight of God.

Peace only comes with silent night,

Quietness rings in my ears

As I sit here alone in the dark.

It is dead silent in these woods,

Too quiet for this time of night.

The animals all have fled,

As my howling echoes towards them.

I search the horizons for anything amiss,

But only darkness and stillness fills my eyes.

No hint of blood or fur is on the air,

So if there is something out there, it's far away.

And yet my ears do still ring

With the howls that I've put behind.

Were they closer than I had thought?

Am I drawing closer towards them?

Or did my howling just seem closer than it was?

Is this lonely life really worth living?

I spend all my time here by myself,

Just tending to my hounds, feeding the beasts.

But, whenever there's a full moon,
I am forced to venture out in the cold night air,
For on those particular nights, the werewolves are out in full force.
The vile creatures prowl about the landscape;
If they are not kept at bay with silver,
They'll feast on man and beast alike.
So I take it upon myself to hunt them down,
To keep the villagers safe and unaware.
For if they found out the dangers that lurk without,
They'd lock themselves up in cages of their own making.
Sometimes I feel like I'm the real monster here.
The villagers have no idea what I've done,
But to keep them safe, I must do what I must.
But that's a thought for another day;
A howl pierces the quiet night air.
It seems the hounds have been drawn to my scent.
I leave, as to not cause a frenzy; already I hear their howls growing louder, nearer.
A chill runs down my spine, and I feel as if eyes are watching me, but I do not stop.
Another howl, this time much closer.
I quicken my pace.
Larger trees give way to smaller shrubs.
I can almost feel them just behind me, gaining on me.
I break into a run.
The pack is gaining on me, I can hear their howls; they're right behind me, ready to take a chunk out of my liver.
The werewolves finally catch up to me and begin to take their share of meat.

NANCY LUCE'S GUIDE TO SELF-CARE
by Nancy Luce, 1872.

1. Bathing:

I recommend taking a bath once a month. First, heat up some water. Boil it if you have to, but get it nice and hot. Get into the bathtub and add the water, nice and slow. When your body has adjusted to the temperature of the water, add a little more. Get all soapy and scrub all your bits! It is important to stay clean, so scrub those pits and cracks! Once you're all soapy clean, rinse off all the soap and get out of the water. If your skin is rough, you can also use a little salt to scrub with, but don't overdo it!

Now you're clean!

You may also wish to wash your hair. This process is much the same as bathing, but remember that your hair is much more sensitive than your skin. Be gentle!

If you have long hair, you may wish to trim the ends every couple months. Use small snips, careful not to take off too much, but don't be timid! Your hair will grow back.

2. Clothing:

Clothing today is so versatile and easy to make that you can easily change your style and look daily if you want! Use color to express your individuality! If you're feeling lazy, you can always throw on a plain brown dress- it's good to have staples in your wardrobe!

You may want to keep a change of clothes with you if you're going out into the wilderness or doing something particularly messy. It's also handy to keep a nightie and robe near your bed so you'll be comfortable and warm on cold, winter nights!

3. Hair:

Many poor folk shave their heads, as hair care is time-consuming and expensive. If you have the time and money for such things, I highly recommend keeping your hair nice and long. It can be styled in many different ways and adds to your charm!

It's also a good idea to keep your hair clean. The best way to do this is with a wash cloth and some water. Start at the roots and work your way to the ends. Remember to keep scrubbing until your hair squeaks- that means it's clean!

Once a month, you may want to take extra time in cleaning your hair. This is important for long haired gals like you! Get a nice conditioner and work it into your roots to the tips of your hair. This will help prevent damage and split ends.

Take time to style your hair! Braids and twists are very popular, so practice these until you get them right! French braids and pigtails are cute on young girls like you. It's important to keep looks simple but elegant; stick with twists and ponies as well. Don't forget to use accessories; a pretty hair bow or a flower can make a boring hairstyle look fantastic.

Long hair tends to get messy. Make sure you keep the long mane under control; tie it up, add hair ornaments, and even carry around a hairbrush! Remember: Hair is your crowning glory. Don't let it turn into a birds' nest.

4. Clothing:

The style of clothing you wear says something about who you are. If you want to make a good impression, try your hand at sewing and alterations. Tailoring is a lost art nowadays, even moreso than poetry, but it's incredibly easy to do with the right tools and a little practice.

You can create your own outfits from scratch by piecing together fabrics and other materials you find or buy. There are thousands of patterns out there for all types of clothing! You want to go for a simple yet elegant style that accentuates your best features.

Dresses are wonderful pieces of clothing. They're easy to put on and look nice in almost any style, from Georgian to modern. Knee-length or longer is preferred for young ladies. Shorter dresses can be worn as well, but ONLY when paired with tights or pants. (Thighs are not attractive.)

Stockings are a great way to cover your legs and keep them warm in wintertime. There are two types of materials: woven and linked. Avoid linked stockings; the seams make bumps that are very noticeable.

Socks are worn looped over or pulled up to your knees. They keep your feet warm and are comfortable, but they get holes easily. Make sure you're adding a few pairs of socks to your yearly shopping list.

Belts can accentuate your best features and bring focus to the waist, one of the most attractive parts of your body!

5. Weapons:

A sword is a traditional weapon used by the Knights of the Silver Order, an ancient order of knights that existed long ago. The swords are magical and cut through nearly anything, although they're short and cannot be used effectively in all situations. It takes a lot of practice for someone to wield one.

A knife is a good weapon for self defense. Although a blade can't be as destructive as a sword, a knife is easier to hide.

A whip is a weapon with a long, skinny piece of leather or braided leather at the end of it. When you swing it, the "cracker" at the end untwists, causing the whip to become tightened and fast. A whip can be dangerous when used by a skilled person.

A gun is a device that shoots metal balls at high speeds out of it. They can be dangerous and deadly if not used carefully.

An axe is a large blade with a short handle wrapped in leather to improve grip. Axes were once the most popular tools for woodcutters. They make good weapons due to their sharpness and power.

A bow and arrow is made of a long, hollow piece of wood with strong, flexible wood glued to the inside forming a curved shape, strung with animal hide and drawn with cord material.

6. Ointments

Ointments and salves are an important part of every modern woman's toilet. There are several different types to choose from:

Sun-tan oil is great for the skin. It prevents wrinkles and dry skin caused by too much sun.

Lip salve contains ingredients to protect and moisturize chapped lips.

Nail polish comes in a huge variety of colors and can also serve as a protective layer for your nails' top layers in case you bite them.

Anti-aging cream firms up wrinkles and gives the skin tone.

Shoe black softens and waterproofs leather. Feet, too! It can also revive older pairs of shoes or boots, and make newer pairs a bit more comfortable.

Anti-perspirant prevents the user from sweating. This is especially helpful for people with stinky sweat.

Tooth whitener makes your teeth nice and shiny.

Optional-Lip gloss makes your lips shinier than using only lip salve.

Black polish is a popular color for nails. It's a shiny, dark grey. Nail polish, black. Shoe black, black. Shoe polish is good for making older shoes' leather softer and waterproof. It can also make new shoes more comfortable to wear.

Tar-and-feathers is a non-lethal ammo for shotguns. They are very hard on the skin and can cause nasty blisters.

Whip is a dangerous melee weapon that is best used by people in excellent physical condition. It is especially effective when used on human targets.

Adhesive tape wraps easily and sticks well to itself, but not to anything else.

Facial creams are good for moisturizing the skin.

7. Sleep

Sleep is important for the body and mind. You feel disoriented and unsure of yourself after not having it for several days. Long-term deprivation can have serious medical consequences.

Beds: You can doze off more efficiently in a bed than, say, on a pile of hay or on the floor of a cell. After a hard day's work, nothing is more welcoming than a soft, pillowy mattress. Many people find themselves dreaming more vividly in an environment like this.

8. Prayers

Praying to the Old Ones is an efficient way of instilling a sense of peace and tranquility in one's mind, even in the most stressful situations. By speaking the incantations to an altar devoted to the Great Old One, you can achieve a state of mental clarity.

Long hours at sea can cause sailors to experience hallucinations and delusions, which manifest as mirages and ghosts among the waves. This phenomenon is known as Seafaring Ghosts. While the visions are benign, they can hinder a captain's judgement and cause paranoia among crew members. Tending to an altar constructed in honor of the Deep Ones can provide some leniency against these effects.

9. Humor.

Humor in modern society is complex. To some, humor is an art form. To others, it's a device to cope with a harsh reality. Sometimes it functions as both. In the world of darkness you've found yourself in, one can never be too sure if a soul you encounter is harboring hostile intent or not. By attempting to find the root of a potential adversary's joy or amusement, you may be able to undermine their capacity for aggression and compel them to leave you alone.

The state of boredom is destructive to the human mind. Prolonged exposure can cause one's thoughts and actions to become increasingly irrational, consuming the victim's capability for clear judgment and positive behavior. Many a mind has been shattered by the tedium of isolation.

10. Teeth Hygiene.

As the old saying goes, one cannot underestimate the importance of oral hygiene. From birth, our society teaches us that daily toothbrushing is imperative to our survival and well-being. Unfortunately, there are some cultures in this world who don't hold to the same standards of cleanliness as we do. These people are the outliers, but they still pop up from time to time, especially when you're at sea. They can harbor infectious diseases and pass them on to you without even realizing it. While this isn't the 15th century, there are no doctors out at sea for hundreds or even thousands of miles. The importance of tooth care is something your ancestors should have instilled in you, but pesky things like "society" and "modern living" made that a bit difficult, so you'll just have to learn the hard way. Stay safe out there!

This is the final message of...

Oh no. Your eyes snap open, pupils fully dilated. You're hyperventilating, breathing faster and faster as you draw air through your flaring nostrils, in and out, in and out. Your body is trembling. Your hands are trembling. Your whole body is trembling. Why is it so dark? Why can't you see anything? You smack your face into the floor again and again and again, whimpering, wailing, shrieking, howling, roaring, begging for death to take you.

After what seems like an eternity but what is, in reality, only a few minutes, you regain some semblance of your faculties. You sit up from the filthy floor and groan out loud in pain.

A DULL MISGIVING

My hens are my only amusement. I speak to them, pray to and for them, write poetry to them, and after feeding out of my hand they roost on and about my bed. I am a poetess, but my literary productions are too deeply involved and deal too extensively with the Unknowable and Ineffable and Unintelligible to appeal to the sympathies of the average reader.

Truly, I have written of the things I have seen and felt, and experienced such emotions that mere mortals cannot grasp nor experience.

My niche has always been here, in this house by this cove. They come to me with their petty demands that I sign away my land, but they will not swerve me from my path. They want to put up more houses and shops in the name of profit, but I will not move from my home.

Unspeakable things burrow under Tyer's Cove. They sleep now. They have not been disturbed. I will not have my sleep disturbed nor my livestock preyed upon by unearthly things from unknown caverns.

But I am running out of time. He will not give me any peace. He is coming soon, the man they call The Butcher, who has all the armies of the world at his command. They say he stands a good chance of winning the island.

I must prepare for that inevitability.

Perhaps the tide of progress that is setting so strongly in at Edgartown may veer to Tisbury. Yet one cannot indulge in any such visions, for in Tisbury we dream more of the past than of the future, and our reveries have no such things as new hotels and horse-cars among them.

Our dreams at Tisbury are more likely to have pixies in them, if not Patagonians, but even then only as the pixies themselves are apt to appear at night when they dance upon our rounds.

Patagonians and the like are poor subjects for night-thoughts--they suggest morning, and impending daylight. They will not do for me and my round tower.

Every house in Tisbury is girt around with trees and shrubs, and as each one was built by some individual for his own dwelling, there is not a particle of uniformity, either in the construction or the position. Some are concealed almost entirely by our neighbors' trees, and to find them you have to penetrate a labyrinth of little alleys winding among plats of vegetables and great clinging vines. One house is built upon a rock, another is stuck on the top of a tall pine tree; one is so completely hidden within a clump of forest trees that you would pass within six feet of it in the twilight without seeing it. That is my favorite one. From every door and every window the pure sea air floods in, and the sunlight sifting through the leaves paints pretty patterns on the floor.

What the neighbors do not know is that the rocks beneath our homes are hollow. The builders of Tyer's Cove made them so, to be refuges in case of an attack. The Indians made them so, and when the island belonged to Old England the patriots made them so when James the Second sent over a crew of butchers to rule the colony in his stead. One must always be prepared in case of the worst.

In the cupboard, behind a row of glass jars of green goo filled with chunks of round, red fruit sits an old blue tin trunk. I keep my most precious treasures in it: a folding telescope; the first edition of Shelley's "Frankenstein" I ever found, with all the original watercolors and an ex libris inscription from Mary herself; a rag doll; Ada's nightgown and brush; my father's flintlock pistol; The Small Book of Sorrows. They weren't safe in the bank when I went to Tethys, and even though they were in the hands of criminals I knew they would be safe with them.

I've been writing in this book for years! It is filled with tales of my murders, and a bit of poetry too. I can't put down everything: I would fill several books like this if I did. The memories flood back so strongly as I write: the wind blowing through my hair, the taste of gall in my mouth, the fear in my enemies' eyes.

Soon I may finish this book, for it is no longer safe to keep it here. I will be ready soon. I am rarely seen out of my house, and trusted even less. Soon they will come for me, the fools in their constabulary blue, armed only with outdated muskets and the finest swords that the brand new US Armory in Harper's Ferry can manufacture. Yet I will be ready for them: my swords are razor sharp, my claws sharper still, and the suit of armor I wear is wrought with silver from the mine I have in California. Soon, I will be finished. I can only hope that one day, someone else finds this book and is moved to pick up my mantle.

After you've re-read this book, I command you to:

I. - PICK UP A SWORD AND DEFEND THY HEN HOUSE

II. - PUT DOWN THE SWORD AND LIVE PEACEABLY AMONG THY ENEMIES

III. - PUT DOWN THE SWORD AND BE KILLED LIKE A SHEEP

IV. - STAY IN THE HOUSE AND PREPARE TO MEET THINE ENEMIES

V. - PUT DOWN THE SWORD AND DIE, UNSATISFIED, BY A LOVED ONES HAND

VI. - PICK UP A BOOK AND ENJOY THY LIBERTY

VII. - PUT DOWN THE SWORD AND BE KILLED ON A POET'S HATRED

VIII. - PICK UP A GUN AND LET SLIP A CORPORAL BULLET

IX. - PICK UP A GUN AND LET SLIP A DULL MISGIVING

Decision Points: You are faced with many decisions. You can look at one, or many, but you cannot look at them all. Most lead to a bad end: only following the right path to the very end will grant you your freedom.

Who is right? The lawmen, coming to arrest you for a crime you didn't commit, who will kill you in an instant if they find you? Or the cloaked man, come to hunt you down for a crime you really did commit, who will offer you absolution if he finds you?

Or are they both right? Will neither of them absolve your sins, and will the evil that courses through your veins never be washed away?

Decide wisely.

AFTERWARD

Don't Miss:
"Nancy Luce and the Foul Smell from Chilmark" –
Book Five of the Nancy Luce: Monster Hunter series!

More hair-raising Nancy Luce adventures
by bestselling author Dr. Charles Banks.

Set for release this August!

ABOUT THE AUTHOR

Dr. Charles E. Banks (1854-1931) was head surgeon of the U.S. Marine Hospital in Vineyard Haven, Mass., from 1889 until 1892. He is known for his three volume publication, "The History of Martha's Vineyard."